The Voic

GABRIEL OKARA w... country of the Niger Delta in Nigeria. He was educated at Government College, Umuahia, and worked as a bookbinder and later as an information officer at Enugu. He has also written plays and features for broadcasting and is known as a poet of outstanding ability. His poetry has appeared regularly in *Black Orpheus*.

The Voice was first published in 1964 and has been described as one of the most memorable novels to have come out of Nigeria.

African writers
available in Fontana

Cameron Duodu	*The Gab Boys*
Obi Egbuna	*Elina*
	Emperor of the Sea
	The Madness of Didi
	The Minister's Daughter
Buchi Emecheta	*The Bride Price*
	Destination Biafra
	Second-Class Citizen
	The Slave Girl
Chukwuemeka Ike	*The Chicken Chasers*
	Expo '77
	The Naked Gods
	The Potter's Wheel
	Sunset at Dawn
	Toads for Supper
Camara Laye	*The African Child*
	A Dream of Africa
	The Guardian of the Word
	The Radiance of the King
Nkem Nwankwo	*My Mercedes is Bigger than Yours*
	Danda
Wole Soyinka	*The Interpreters*
Adaora Lily Ulasi	*The Man from Sagamu*

The Voice

Gabriel Okara

Fontana/Collins

First published by André Deutsch Ltd 1964
First issued in Fontana Paperbacks 1973
Second impression October 1983

Made and printed in Great Britain by
William Collins Sons & Co. Ltd, Glasgow

TO GEOFF AND FIN
PAUL AND PAT

ONE

Some of the townsmen said Okolo's eyes were not right, his head was not correct. This they said was the result of his knowing too much book, walking too much in the bush, and others said it was due to his staying too long alone by the river.

So the town of Amatu talked and whispered; so the world talked and whispered. Okolo had no chest, they said. His chest was not strong and he had no shadow. Everything in this world that spoiled a man's name they said of him, all because he dared to search for *it*. He was in search of *it* with all his inside and with all his shadow.

Okolo started his search when he came out of school and returned home to his people. When he returned home to his people, words of the coming thing, rumours of the coming thing, were in the air flying like birds, swimming like fishes in the river. But Okolo did not join them in their joy because what was there was no longer there and things had no more roots. So he started his search for *it*. And this stopped the Elders from slapping their thighs in joy because of the coming thing.

Why should Okolo look for *it*, they wondered. Things have changed, the world has turned and they are now the Elders. No one in the past has asked for *it*. Why should Okolo expect to find *it* now that they are the Elders? No, he must stop his search. He must not spoil their pleasure.

So Chief Izongo spoke at the gathering of Elders and the Elders, in their insides, turned these spoken words over and over and looked to see the path they would take to avoid this stinking thing. They turned over the spoken words and sent messengers to Okolo to ask him to cease forthwith his search for *it*.

So the messengers, three messengers, set forth on their timid road for Okolo's house. They walked slowly and then faster, and soon one of them hit his foot against a stone.

First messenger : 'My right foot has hit against a stone.'

Second messenger : 'Is it good or bad?'

First messenger (*Solemnly*) : 'It's bad.'

Second messenger : 'Bad? My right foot is good to me.'

Third messenger : 'Your nonsense words stop. These things have meaning no more. So stop talking words that create nothing.'

First messenger : 'To me there is meaning. My right foot always warns me.'

Second messenger : 'To me too there is meaning. If my left foot against something hits as I walk, it's a warning be.'

Third messenger (*With contempt*) : 'Nonsense.'

First messenger : 'Listen not to him. He speaks this way always because he passed standard six. Because he passed standard six his ears refuseth nothing, his inside refuseth nothing like a dustbin.'

Third messenger : 'Your spoken words I call nothing. What I say is, things have changed, so change.'

First messenger (*Spits on the ground*) : 'Hear his creating words – things changeth. Ha, ha, ha . . . change, change. He always of change speaks. Ha, ha, ha. What is the whiteman's word, the parable you always say . . . "the old order changeth"? I forget the rest, you always. . . .'

Third messenger (*Angrily*) : 'Shut your mouth. You know nothing.'

First messenger (*Also angrily*) : 'Me know nothing? Me know nothing? Because I went not to school I have no bile, I have no head? Me know nothing? Then answer me this. Your hair was black black be, then it became white like a white cloth and now it is black black be more than blackness. The root, what is it? You keep quiet. Answer me. I know nothing, you say.'

Second messenger (*Throws his eyes back and front, left and right and speaks with lowered voice*): 'Speak of this thing no more. The ears of Amatu are open. If this the ears of Izongo enters, we will fall from our jobs. You know this yourselves. As for me (*shrugs his shoulders*), if the world turns this way I take it; if it turns another way I take it. Any way the world turns I take it with my hands. I like sleep and my wife and my one son, so I do not think.'

Third messenger: 'You know not what you speak.'

First messenger (*Raising his voice*): 'He is raising himself to the eye of the sky.'

Second messenger (*Lowering his voice to the ground*): 'Talk not like this, hold yourself. I tell you, yourself hold before this thing a big thing turns.'

These teaching words their ears entered and their insides entered. So they locked every word carefully in their insides as they silently walked towards Okolo's house without their mouths opening.

It was the day's ending and Okolo by a window stood. Okolo stood looking at the sun behind the tree tops falling. The river was flowing, reflecting the finishing sun, like a dying away memory. It was like an idol's face, no one knowing what is behind. Okolo at the palm trees looked. They were like women with hair hanging down, dancing, possessed. Egrets, like white flower petals strung slackly across the river, swaying up and down, were returning home. And, on the river, canoes were crawling home with bent backs and tired hands, paddling. A girl with only a cloth tied around her waist and the half-ripe mango breasts, paddled, driving her paddle into the river with a sweet inside.

Okolo left the window and went to his table. He opened a book and read. He read the book without being aware of passing time until night fell and closed the eye of the sky. To the window he went once more and looked at the night. The moon was an about-to-break moon. A vague circle of light surrounded it, telling a dance was going on up or down river. Across the moon's face and the dance circle, menacing dark clouds idled past, casting shadow after shadow on the river. Larger and darker clouds, some to frowning faces, grimacing faces changing, were skulking past without the moon's ring, suffocating the stars until they too lost themselves in the threatening conformity of the dark cloud beyond.

Shuffling feet turned Okolo's head to the door. He saw three men standing silent, opening not their mouths. 'Who are you people be?' Okolo asked. The people opened not their mouths. 'If you are coming-in people be, then come in.' The people opened not their mouths. 'Who are you?' Okolo again asked, walking to the men. As Okolo closer to the men walked, the men quickly turned and ran out.

The root of this Okolo knew not as the root of many many happening things in the town. So wonder held him and moved him to the door. Okolo saw a crowd, a crowd of men, women and children talking, whispering, and three men talking and gesticulating in front. Wonder again moved Okolo out of his door and as he closer walked to the crowd, somebody moved by fear stuck to the ground. Women grabbed their children and ran. If the saliva from the mouth of one whose head is not correct enters one's mouth, one's head also becomes not correct. So they ran and some men too who had no chest or shadow in them also ran. But the three men in front trembled first and then stood resolutely, facing Okolo.

Okolo seeing the messengers, recognized them and questioned them. But the men, in spite of their grim faces, opened not their mouths. The remaining crowd hushed. The silence passed silence. The three messengers faced Okolo, opening not their mouths. A man from

10

the back of the crowd pushed his way to the messengers. The four of them put their heads together while with their eyes they looked at Okolo. They put their heads together for awhile and walked towards Okolo, as if stalking an animal. And Okolo stood looking. They moved nearer. Okolo stood. They moved nearer and suddenly, pounced on Okolo. Okolo and the men fell to the ground. Hands clawed at him, a thousand hands, the hands of the world. Okolo twisted, struggled and kicked with all his shadow, with all his life and, to his astonishment, he saw himself standing free. He ran. Running feet followed. He ran. A million pursuing feet thundered after him. He ran past his house without knowing and ran into another. A woman giving suck to her baby screamed. Out Okolo sprang and ran. The running feet came nearer, the caring-nothing feet of the world. Okolo turned a corner and nearly ran into a boy and girl standing with hands holding each other. They did not look at him. He turned a corner. A dog barked at him. Okolo ran. He was now at the ending of the town. Only one hut was left and beyond it the mystery of the forest. Okolo ran and as he ran past, a voice held him. 'Come in,' it said. 'Come in quickly.' In Okolo went, instinctively and in the gloom, stood panting. Outside, the dog barked, the pursuing feet of the world stopped and the shout of triumph from the ground reached the eye of the sky and all the town shook. As the shout shook the town like a cannon blast, fear entered Okolo and he thought of escape through the hole, the sole window at the back. But a hand reached him from the dark void. 'Stay quiet,' the darkness whispered, 'Nothing they will do to you.' Next, Okolo saw the mat covering the door move aside.

Faces, a mass of faces glistening with sweat in the moonlight stood, talking, arguing. Grim faces like the dark mysterious forest afire with flies. Then a shadow blocked his view, then silence. And a voice clear and cool like a glass of water, from the standing shadow sallied forth.

'What is it? What again do you want of me? What do you want of a witch?'

'We want nothing of you,' a voice came from the crowd. 'We want nothing of you. We want only the man you keep in your house.'

'I keep no one. Why should I any of you keep who called me a witch and have kept me away from the town? Why should I any of you keep? Leave me alone. Go your ways,' the standing shadow strongly spoke without fear.

As the standing shadow spoke thus, a stronger voice came from the crowd. 'We go our ways? You cannot speak thus to us. Know that you are a witch be. You couldn't thus speak to us in the old times. Even now . . .'

'Come and take me and hang me as in the old times they used to do. Come and take me,' went forth the challenge from the standing shadow.

'Give us our man,' shouted a voice.

'Which man you want of me?' asked Tuere with a strong inside.

'Give us Okolo.'

'Okolo? Why should I keep him? Is he not one of you?'

'Argue not with her,' said a voice. 'Let's enter the house and bring him out.'

'I say I keep no one. If you say the man you want is in my house, come in and take him,' said Tuere with a steady inside.

'You say he entered the forest?' asked a voice.

'I said not so. Accuse me not of what I said not,' she said.

'You heard not his footsteps?' asked another voice.

'I am used to only bad footsteps. So I only heard bad footsteps.'

'You say bad footsteps you heard?'

'Yes. Bad footsteps coming out of people's insides.'

'I say argue not with her. How Okolo entered her house I saw with this my two eyes. I was in the front be.

Let's go in and drag him out,' said a voice from the crowd impatiently.

When this last man spoke thus, Tuere walked forward. And as Tuere advanced the men in the crowd's front moved back.

'Stand!' a voice from the crowd's back urged. 'Stand! She cannot do anything. We are all church people. We all know God. She cannot do anything to us.'

'Is it you who speak thus?' said Tuere. 'Is it you, Seitu? It was you who first called me a witch and then others followed you to call me a witch. Now you say nothing I can do to you. When did your belief in the powers of witchcraft finish in your inside? You say you are a know-God man be. Come and enter my house.'

'You can nothing do,' said Seitu from the crowd's back.

'I say argue not with her,' said the one who said this before. 'Our time is finishing.'

'I see. . . . You know time finishes. Yet when my father's time finished and he went away, you people put it on my head. And when the time of my mother finished and she went away, you said I filled her with witchcraft. Whose time finishes not? Whose time finishes not? Our time is finishing just as the time of some of your relations, your fathers and mothers finished and they went to the land of the dead. You did not kill them with witchcraft. But it is I who with witchcraft killed my father and my mother. Yes, you say I am a witch, so I am a witch be.' The standing shadow with all her inside spoke and watched their reaction as a school mistress would the reaction of her pupils after delivering a few homilies. The crowd moved backwards and forwards, not knowing what to do.

Inside the hut Okolo stood, hearing all the spoken words outside and speaking with his inside. He spoke with his inside to find out why this woman there behaved thus. He knew her story only too well. She had been a girl of unusual habits, keeping to herself and speaking to herself. She did not flirt with boys though she had a hunger-killing beauty. So it was in the insides of everyone that perhaps she had not the parts of a woman. They did not, because of these her strange behaviours, call her a witch. They openly called her a witch when her mother and father died one after the other within a few weeks and after every young man who proposed to her died one after the other. All these Okolo remembered. He also remembered how in a circle of strong eyes and strong faces she stood being accused of taking witchcraft to kill her father and mother. They then from the town drove her. His inside then smelled bad for the town's people and for himself for not being fit to do anything on her behalf. But this feeling in his inside had slowly, slowly died with each dying year under the mysterious might of tradition. And now wonder held him for her protecting him. He was a part of the society that had disgraced and rejected her. But now she was protecting him from the very society.

So it was with wrong-doing-filled inside that he moved to the door and peered out. He did not deserve this of her. Shame, like rain, fell on him and touched his bones. But as he peered out the crowd was moving backwards and forwards, talking and arguing.

'Come forward if you can come,' Tuere challenged.

'You can do nothing to us,' said Seitu still at the back of the crowd, making himself the voice of the crowd.

Okolo wanted to go out but he had two opposing voices speaking in his inside. One said 'go' and the other said 'stay', and before he could decide on which to obey Tuere threw another challenge at the crowd. 'You refuse to come, you who are only strong in a crowd.

'We are know-God people. You can do nothing. Just bring our man,' replied Seitu from the crowd's back.

Tuere standing straight and walking towards the crowd, said, 'Then I to you come'. As she said thus and moved slowly towards the crowd, the crowd moved back and the people turned their backs, including Seitu, the voice of the people, and ran. They ran with the backs of their feet touching the back of their heads. Who would want to die of itches? No one. So they ran with all their insides and with all their shadows. Tuere stood watching the bad footsteps dying away and smiled the first smile that had come out of her mouth since she was stuck with the name of witch and was ostracized.

Okolo wanted to go out but at that one moment Tuere turned and walked towards the hut. He wanted to get out but his inside told him that would be the lowest ingratitude, an ingratitude that would be worse than disowning one's parents. His inside did not agree with him. So he moved back into the gloom of the hut and waited.

Presently, Tuere stepped silently in and put the mat over the door. And the hut became dark with darkness exceeding darkness. Though they were only a few paces apart, Okolo could not see her. They stood thus silent without each other seeing, listening to their insides, listening to the darkness. Then suddenly Okolo heard walking feet. Feet walking towards the dying embers at the hearth. Then he saw the embers move and glow like a new-appearing sun or a going-down sun. Then he saw splinters of firewood drop on the embers. And then he heard her trying to blow the embers to living flames. She blew, blew and blew, but the embers only glowed not responding like a god more sacrifice demanding. They only glowed showing a face intent in supplication. She continued to blow, her breath coming in soft gusts. Then a token flame shot up momentarily and died.

Okolo stood watching and speaking to his inside. How many years has she killed tending the dying embers of her fire with her breath and shadow and wishes and remembrances?

As Okolo stood thus speaking with his inside, a voice entered his inside asking him to bring some firewood from the corner of the hut. With a start, he moved towards the corner with hands extended in front.

Soon his hands touched the wall. Then he lowered them slowly until he touched the splinters of firewood propped against the wall. He took them and moved back. As he moved back unseen hands took the firewood from his hands and crossed them on the embers. Then there were more blowings. Then suddenly a twin flame shot up. The twin flame going into one another and becoming one, grew long and short, spread, twisted and danced, devouring the essence of the firewood like passion. And the face of Tuere was satisfaction, for her breath and shadow had gone into the flame. She remained kneeling before the dancing flame with face intent, looking at the flame, looking at what is behind the flame, the root of the flame. She remained kneeling, then slowly rose to her feet, turned and faced Okolo. And before Okolo could open his mouth to thank her, she spoke.

'How do you expect to find *it*? How do you expect to find *it* when everybody has locked up his inside?'

Okolo did as if to speak.

'How do I know this, you want to ask me? I know I hear every happening thing in the town even though I am locked up here in this hut. How or where do you think you will find *it* when everybody surface-water-things tell, when things have no more root? How do you expect to find *it* when fear has locked up the insides of the low and the insides of the high are filled up with nothing but yam? Stop looking for *it*. Stop suffering yourself.'

'I cannot stop,' Okolo with whisper whisper spoke. 'I cannot stop this thing. I must find *it*. It is there. I am the voice from the locked up insides which the Elders, not wanting the people to hear, want to stop me. Their insides are smelling bad and hard at me, but. . . .'

'Ssh!' Tuere hushed Okolo, cocking her head. 'I hear coming footsteps.' Okolo listened and he also heard the coming footsteps, the knowing-nothing footsteps, coming!

TWO

The knowing-nothing footsteps, the bad footsteps, kept coming. They came to the door and stopped.

'I'll go and meet them,' Okolo said and rose but Tuere reached the door before him and even as she pushed aside the mat covering the door wickedness issued forth from Chief Izongo's mouth to her.

'Tuere,' he called her. 'Deliver Okolo to me or we burn your hut to the ground.'

'I do not hear what you say,' said Tuere with a straight voice as she stood straight like a bamboo pole in front of the crowd.

Izongo laughed a laugh that did not reach his inside and the crowd swayed this way and that way like tall grass being swayed by a gust of wind.

'What you say does not enter my inside,' she said, after looking at the moving faces of the crowd and at the eyes of Chief Izongo. 'Go away. Nobody I have to give you,' she said and turned to enter her hut, but Chief Izongo's voice held her.

'We know Okolo is in one dark corner there covering himself with darkness. If you refuse to bring him to me we will burn your house to the ground,' Chief Izongo said with a stone voice and the words fell like gravel from a tipper.

Tuere turned and faced Chief Izongo and the crowd, her inside smelling with anger.

'Doesn't shame fall on your head, you man without a chest, for saying you want to burn a woman's house down to the ground? If you are a male man be with a strong chest, come and take him,' she challenged standing straighter than straightness. As she finished speaking thus with her breathing not reaching ground be-

17

cause of her smelling anger, Okolo suddenly spoke from her side.

'Here I am,' he said with a voice cool as cool water. 'Do not touch her. If you want me I will come but you must tell me the bottom of it.'

'Do not ask the bottom of things,' Chief Izongo said after laughing a surface-water laugh. 'Do not ask the bottom of things, my friend. I want you and that is the end.'

'You have to tell me the bottom of it,' Okolo insisted.

'Do not ask the bottom of things. I have told you so many times. Now let me give you some teaching words,' Chief Izongo said lowering his voice. 'Listen. Asking the bottom of things in this town will take you no place. Hook this with your little finger. Put it into your inside's box and lock it up.'

'Your teaching words do not enter my inside. If it is a thing with a good bottom why not send a messenger?' Okolo asked.

'You mean my wanting you has a bad bottom,' Chief Izongo said, laughing a laugh that was no laughter. 'Was it not you who one day gave us some teaching words from your books which say that what I eat may be a man-killing medicine to another person? My wanting you may be man-killing medicine to you but it is the best food for my body.'

He then looked at Okolo and laughed. 'I have held him with his own teaching words,' he said turning to the crowd and raising his hands in triumph. He turned again to Okolo.

'If it is man-killing medicine to you, then it is bad more than badness which to me is nothing. You cannot fell a fallen tree. I know the world is now bad but your coming with me will not make it bad more than badness. So come quietly,' so Chief Izongo ended with the crowd murmuring approval.

'I will not come,' Okolo said with his shadow.

'Then I will burn the hut to the ground,' Chief

Izongo threatened.

'You have a very ugly inside,' Okolo said looking at him with strong eyes.

'Look, my valuable friend,' Chief Izongo started in a low voice. 'In this town you and your followers alone think so and you are only two. The whole town is at my back. So what you say will do nothing to me.' He ended in a very high voice.

'Why do you want me then? All the town is here. Say what you want to say.'

'Since you are asking the bottom of this thing with all your strength like a little girl trying to lift a big basket of yams, I will put my hand for you. Now open your ears and listen.' Chief Izongo paused. He looked at Okolo and then at the crowd. He then looked at Okolo again, his eyes moving slowly from Okolo's feet up to Okolo's eyes, and remained there.

'Your head is not correct!' Chief Izongo shouted at Okolo.

'Me, my head not correct?' Okolo said laughing in disbelief.

'I know that you do not agree as one that palm-wine has held does not agree that palmwine has held him; or as one who sleeps at a meeting does not agree that he sleeps. So whether you agree or do not agree means nothing to me because one whose head is not correct never agrees that his head is not correct,' said Chief Izongo closing his mouth as if nothing would come out of it again.

'My head is as clear and cool like rain water,' said Okolo. 'So if you want me for another thing, say so without fear.'

'You think I fear?' Chief Izongo spoke, his inside smelling with anger. 'I have given you plenty of time to come. If you waste more time wrestling with me with words I will burn the hut down.'

So saying, he waved his hand and some people with torches approached the hut. Okolo let fall a deep breath.

'I am coming,' he said and stood looking at the people. Then he turned to Tuere standing by his side. 'Thank you,' he said simply and walked to Chief Izongo, brushing aside the begging hands of Tuere.

The people snapped at him like hungry dogs snapping at bones. They carried him in silence like the silence of ants carrying a crumb of yam or fish bone. Then they put him down and dragged him past thatch houses that in the dark looked like pigs with their snouts in the ground; pushed and dragged him past mud walls with pitying eyes; pushed and dragged him past concrete walls with concrete eyes; pushed and dragged him along the waterside like soldier ants with their prisoner. They pushed and dragged him in panting silence, shuffling silence, broken only by an owl hooting from the darkness of the orange tree in front of Chief Izongo's house. Okolo became tired. His mouth opened slackly and the breath came out without reaching his chest. His feet belonged to him no longer. But his head was clear and his inside was unruffled like water in a glass. He spoke with his inside :

'I am moving round and round caught in a whirlpool of hate and greed and I smell the smell of hate in their sweat glistening on their backs. . . .'

On and on they pushed and dragged him. Round and round they went with their blind feet. This way they turned and that way they turned like a dog with a piece of bone looking for a corner. Nobody talked, nobody whispered. They pushed and dragged him in tramping silence with buzzing mosquitoes. . . .

A fly stood on his nose. Okolo turned on his side and continued to sleep. Another stood on his ear. He shook his head. It flew off and stood on the ear. He turned and slept on his back. The fly stood on his eyes. He shook his head. The fly flew off. He was now between sleeping and waking, thinking and not thinking, floating between sky and earth. The fly settled on his mouth. He tried to move his hand but his hand would not move! Then suddenly fear opened his eyes wide, in spite of his strong chest, and he came down to earth. And as he gazed at the ceiling, he saw yesterday's night passing before his eyes. Okolo shut his eyes to shut off the nightmare and spoke with his inside. . . .

A fly stood on his face. He tried to lift his hands but they would not move so he shook his head and the fly flew off. He opened his eyes and rolled to the edge of the bed and throwing over his feet he sat up. He looked at his hands. They were bound with a rope. Could this be a real thing? But the rope told him it was real. He tugged at his hands. The rope would not give. He stared at his wrists. A fly hovered and stood on the rope. It screwed its head this way and that way and rubbed its forelegs as if washing its hands of the squabbles of man.

Okolo with his head on his chest sat talking to his inside. He did not know for how long he sat thus when footsteps entered his inside and raised his head. He saw approaching from the door, his two friends.

'What is behind your coming?' he asked as they came before him. They ignored Okolo's questioning words and one said, with a chestful voice, that Chief Izongo wanted him.

'Why does he want me again? What he has done to me has not filled his belly?'

His friends shifted from one foot to the other as if they were standing on a hot ground and opened not their mouths.

'Untie my hands,' he said. His friends' eyes went up to the ceiling.

'We are waiting,' one said.

'Tell me the bottom of everything,' Okolo said with a soft voice. 'We have been friends for a long time since we were children so tell me the bottom of everything. There is nobody here.'

'We are waiting,' his friends said together, their

voices sounding like the sound of a stone falling on stone.

Okolo sat silent looking at his hands. He decided to try again.

'You are men with strong chests. Why do you fear Chief Izongo? He is a man like you and me. I know that you are doing this thing not because you like it but because you are walking with fear behind you, pushing you as you pushed me yesterday. Why do you allow fear to so own you?'

'Chief Izongo wants you and we are waiting,' his friends said, still gazing at the ceiling.

Okolo let fall a big breath and standing up, led the way out in silence with his friends walking behind him.

Outside, he walked strongly with no fear in his feet and no fear in his inside, casting bad eyes at him and from dark interiors of houses people looked at him with Chief Izongo's eyes and behind him walked his friends, walking with Chief Izongo's feet.

On seeing Okolo standing in his front, Chief Izongo with a jug of palmwine in his hand, laughed loud and long and then suddenly stopped. The Elders around him all looked at him.

'Laugh!' he commanded, and the Elders opened their mouths showing their teeth like grinning masks and made a noise that could hardly pass for laughter.

'Why are my hands tied?' Okolo asked, with his voice as strong as stone.

'Hear him,' Izongo said with his lips on the edge of the jug. He took a sip of palmwine. 'Hear him,' he repeated after swallowing the palmwine. 'Always asking questions. Questions will take you nowhere. I keep telling you these teaching words.' He looked at the Elders and they nodded their heads vigorously in agreement.

'Untie my hands. This is no question. All I ask from you is let me be free.' At this Izongo laughed and the Elders this time taking the cue also laughed.

'I am sure it is with the eye of sleep that I am seeing

all this. I am sure I am seeing with dream's eye,' Okolo talked aloud in his inside.

'Yes, indeed, you have been dreaming since you came and I've been trying to wake you since yesterday,' Izongo said with a wise voice and looked at the Elders. They nodded their heads and mumbled their agreement.

'How are you going to wake me from my dream?' Okolo asked.

'Ah!' Izongo exclaimed with his hands raised high. 'The boy's head is becoming correct. I will answer this because it will do you good. I will answer this question not only by words but also by deed!' Then he took a long time sipping his palmwine and then looked at his Elders one by one.

'Did I say by deed?' he asked, and some of the Elders shook their heads, others nodded in agreement and yet others tried to do both, resulting in a confusion of heads bobbing and swaying from side to side like the heads of puppets.

An Elder, Abadi, sitting by the side of Chief Izongo suddenly stood up. He was the next man to Izongo and, to speak the straight thing, he was Izongo's adviser. Abadi looked at his fellow Elders with angry eyes. And the Elders looked at him with fear in their eyes. Then Abadi began to speak in English, as he usually did on similar occasions.

'This is an honourable gathering led by an honourable leader,' Abadi began and paused. Chief Izongo looked at the Elders and they shouted, clapped their hands and stamped their feet in applause.

'A leader and chief the like of which we've not seen or heard of in Amatu, nay, in the whole country. A moment ago our most honourable leader asked a simple question requiring a simple answer. Yet some of us hesitated, others did not know what to say. Perhaps they did so in a moment of forgetfulness. But forgetfulness in an occasion like this when we are going to take momentous decisions is barefaced ingratitude. . . .'

Chief Izongo looked at the Elders and they shifted on their seats. 'What could you have been without our leader? Some of you were mere fishermen, palm cutters and some of you were nothing in the days of the imperialists. But now all of you are Elders and we are managing our own affairs and destinies. So you and I know what is expected of us, and that is, we must toe the party line. We must have discipline and self-sacrifice in order to see this fight through to its logical conclusion.

'Our duty, therefore, is clear. We must support our most honourable leader. And on my part, I here and now declare my most loyal and unswerving support and pledge my very blood to the cause.

'That thing there (pointing at Okolo), we've heard nothing but of him since a year ago when he returned. Why? It is all because he attended a secondary school and thinks he is educated. Is he the only person who is educated in Amatu, granting that he is educated? I am not given to blowing my own trumpet (no one blew his louder than himself at the least opportunity which he often created for himself) but for this once I will. I have been to England, America and Germany and attended the best universities in these places and have my MA, PhD. . . .'

'You have your MA, PhD, but you have not got *it*,' Okolo interrupted him, also speaking in English. All eyes, including Chief Izongo's left Abadi and settled on Okolo. Abadi's face became twisted in rage but he held himself.

'As I was saying, I have my MA, PhD degrees,' he continued and all eyes left Okolo and settled again on Abadi. 'But I, my very humble self, knew where my services were most required and returned to Amatu to fight under the august leadership of our most honourable leader. I cannot therefore stand by when I see our cause about to be jeopardized by anyone.

'Okolo is a coward. If he were not why did he hide

in Tuere's house? Why did he skulk there instead of coming to face the people like a man?'

'So I am no longer mad but a coward,' Okolo again interrupted. All eyes left Abadi and settled on Okolo. Abadi's face again became twisted in rage but he again held himself. 'You know Abadi, that I am neither mad nor a coward.'

'It makes no difference,' Abadi returned. 'We are fighting a great fight and this is not the time to split hairs.'

'Whom are you fighting against?' Okolo again interrupted him. 'Are you not simply making a lot of noise because it is the fashion in order to share in the spoils. You are merely making a show of straining to open a door that is already open. You go and sleep over this,' Okolo said.

'You mark your words,' Abadi said, furious, and his inside began to stink with anger. 'You mark your words. I am going to make you regret this. Why did you skulk in Tuere's house instead of coming to face the people? You should have still been in there hiding if not for the unparalleled gallantry of our leader who brought you running out like a rat. Listen not to him, fellow Elders. His mouth is foul. You and I are comrades in arms and we must see this thing through to its logical conclusion. So let us with one voice answer the question that our leader has put before us a short while ago. We are in a democracy and everyone has the right to express any opinion. But we have to think what our leader has done for us.'

As Abadi ended, there arose a great shout of applause, feet-stamping and hand-clapping. In the midst of this Chief Izongo rose from his seat and stood before the Elders, a thing he had not done before, to speak. As he stood the applause gradually died down until one solitary handclap marked its end. Then with his voice quavering with emotion he began to speak in the vernacular.

'You have first heard the spoken words of Abadi and they have entered your ears. He spoke in English and many words missed our ears while many entered our ears. We will not blame him for that for, who among us will not speak thus with such big book learning. This house will not contain the books he has read. So with a man like him sitting at my right hand side there will be no fear in my inside and my chest will be as strong as stone even if the world falls on my head. So do not allow fear to enter your insides so long as you, the representative of the people, are with us. I will speak no further as our highest son has spoken everything. Now, a little time ago I asked a question as soft as water. I do not know whether I said I would answer Okolo's questions by deed. But I feel I said not so. Everybody forgets things even myself (when convenient) especially as we have taken much palmwine. Even I, Chief Izongo, who you think knows everything, forgets things. So I merely asked you to remind me, but you too were not sure of what my spoken words were. Now I want to ask the question again. On an important matter like this there should be no different voice. All the voices must be one as we have a "collective responsibility", as our highest son says. And to show that there is nothing else in your insides you will your hands raise when I ask the question again. Anyone who raises not his hand I know is not one of us. Now this is my questioning word : Did I say I was going to answer Okolo's question by deed?'

Hands flew up with the precision of drilling soldiers even before Chief Izongo went halfway through his questioning words. Some both hands raised and, one who thought his hands went up before any other waved them so as to catch Chief Izongo's eyes. But Chief Izongo's eyes were not for those he had put into his bag. Who, he thought in his inside, was his last obstacle was in his front standing and the way he looked at Okolo seemed as if he wanted to look him to death.

With his eyes still on Okolo he sat slowly down and ordered the palmwine to be passed round.

With smile smile in his mouth, Okolo looked at Izongo and fear snaked towards Izongo's inside and he gulped down a mouthful of palmwine. So when Okolo said with smile smile in his mouth that he would keep his thoughts in his inside if his hands were untied Chief Izongo's jug stopped at his lips. The Elders also stopped talking. Chief Izongo stared at Okolo and then whispered into the ears of Abadi. Then Abadi in turn whispered into Chief Izongo's ears.

'Keeping your thoughts in your inside alone will not do,' Chief Izongo said grinning. 'Your hands will only be untied if you agree to be one of us.'

'No!' Okolo said. 'No, never!'

Wonder held Izongo, held Abadi, and held all the Elders. They looked at each other. Izongo his head shook vigorously like a stunned man trying to clear his head.

As wonder held them so, Okolo threw his back at them and walked away. But he had gone only a little way when running feet he heard, coming behind him. But he did not look back. He walked on. Then he heard the owners of the running feet calling his name. But he only walked on. He heard the running feet almost touching his heels and he heard their breathing. Hands fell on his shoulders. Okolo then stopped.

'Izongo says you come back,' said one of the messengers with his breath going up and down like the piston of a railway engine. Okolo turned without any spoken word and walked to the presence of Izongo.

'I am – I mean – we are soft-hearted people, soft like water,' Izongo said, raising his eyes to the eye of the sky as if trying to see the root of nature's wonders. 'Our insides are soft like water even if you say our insides are filled with stone. Our eyes too are soft and they cannot fall on suffering. We have been turning it even in our insides since you threw your back at us and left. Our highest son, Abadi, has been telling me an English saying, which I agree fits you, and that saying is that when I do not see you, you will not be in my inside.' He brought his eyes from the eye of the sky and focused them hard on Okolo.

'You must leave this town. It will pain our insides too much to see you suffer. We are a soft people and even now if you agree to join us, we untie your hands and you will have no need to knock your head against stone as you are doing now.'

Izongo looked at his adviser for approval and he got it from him with several nods of his head. All the Elders also nodded their heads. But Okolo looking at them said in his inside that his spoken words would only break against them as an egg would against a stone. So he once more threw his back at them and walked away.

As Okolo entered his house he saw Tebeowei, one of the Elders looking at some old newspapers.

'Sit down Okolo. Nobody sent me,' he said as he saw Okolo's questioning look. 'I was not at the meeting place.'

Okolo went and sat on his bed, the only chair having been occupied by his visitor. Tebeowei looked at his palm and while rubbing out some invisible things started to speak.

'This thing you are doing is too heavy for you,' he said. 'I went to school only a little, but I have killed many many more years in this world than you have. You cannot get anything in this world if you do things like this. These happening things make my inside bitter, perhaps more bitter than yours. But there is nothing I alone or you and I can do to change their insides. It is a bad spirit that is entering everybody and if you do not allow it to get you, they say it's you that has it. So I just sit down and look. If they say anything, I agree. If they do anything, I agree, since they do not take yam out of my mouth. The teaching thing I want to say is that; change and do as others are doing.' He ended and raising his eyes from his palm, looked at Okolo.

Okolo too from the floor lifted his eyes and looked at Tebeowei.

'How can I change my inside?' he said. 'The chair you are sitting on now is made of Abura, a cheap soft wood. Not so?'

'Yes.'

'Well, what will you call a person who says it is made of Iroko?'

'Perhaps he does not know.'

'I mean a person who knows Abura and Iroko. What will you call him?'

'A person who speaks not the straight thing.'

'I know it is Abura and when another person who also knows it is Abura tells the people it is Iroko should I also agree that it is Iroko?'

'In this world things are not like this,' Tebeowei said, looking at his palm once more. 'I see in my inside that your spoken words are true and straight. But you see it in your inside that we have no power to do anything. The spirit is powerful. So it is they who get the spirit that are powerful, and the people believe with their insides whatever they are told. Everything in this world has changed. The world is no longer straight. So if a person turns his palms down I also turn mine down. If he turns them up, opens them and shows them to the eye of the sky, I also turn mine up and show them to the eye of the sky. So turn this over in your inside and do as we do so that you will have a sweet inside like us.'

Okolo stood up and walked round and round the room like an animal in a cage.

'To change my inside and allow what you say to enter can never be a happening thing,' he said at last. 'Do you think a person can his inside change like you change a loin cloth?'

Okolo went and sat on his bed.

'If you put a black paint over a white paint, does it

mean there is no white paint? Under the black paint the white paint is still there and it will show when the black paint is rubbed off. That's the thing I am doing – trying to rub off the black paint. Our fathers' insides always contained things straight. They did straight things. Our insides were also clean and we did the straight things until the new time came. We can still sweep the dirt out of our houses every morning.'

'But the heap of dirt is more than one man's strength, Okolo. It may bury you.'

'But we must start clearing, even if it is only by basketfuls. Chief Izongo does not want me to do even that.'

'I know, Okolo, but you must see the fact of the new time. Everybody's inside is now filled with money, cars, and concrete houses and money is being scattered all around. If any falls at my feet, I stoop and pick it up. If I don't and kick it away, I will be called a know-nothing man and I will be kicked away.'

'But I cannot stoop to pick up such things. Let my hands remain tied. Let me have no money, no friends, no house, no clothes. I like it so.'

'How are you going to remain like this in this town?'

'Has it not entered your ears?'

'What is it?'

'Chief Izongo has put a law that I must leave the town.'

'Where will you go?'

'I am going to Sologa. There, my inside tells me, I will find persons whose insides are like mine.'

'You think so?' said Tebeowei with a knowing smile. 'I stayed and worked there for many many years. I think I killed twenty years in Sologa. Things are worse there and a person like you cannot stay there unless you want to be a beggar. It's dog eat dog there in Sologa.'

'Where else can I go? That is the place I think will enter my inside. Will Izongo be there too?'

'No, but people like him are in Sologa like ants.'

'But where can I go? I must leave this town.'

'Well, I have spoken many teaching words but they have not entered your ears. Maybe the chicken's teaching words will. The chicken says when you are in a new town stand with only one foot, for where you stand may be a grave.' With this Tebeowei rose from his chair. 'May we live to see tomorrow,' he said gravely.

'Yes, may we live to see tomorrow,' Okolo responded. Tebeowei threw his back at Okolo and left.

Okolo did not move from his bed. There he remained talking with his inside until sun down. Nobody sees what he sees. His talking seems to him throwing words away like one throws money into the river. That's what they think. But they do not see it in their insides that words and money are not the same thing. Money may be lost for ever but words, teaching words, are the same in any age. Some of these teaching words are as true today as they were centuries ago. They may be given different meaning to suit the new times but the root is the same. He will continue to speak the straight thing at all times, though Woyengi knows, it is the hardest thing to do in these new times. But continue he will, so long as they do not sew his mouth up with needle and thread. . . .

As he spoke thus in his inside and his ears listening to his inside he saw a figure slip in at the door. In spite of himself his body became stiff but when he heard his name called in a loud whisper his breath reached the floor. It was Tuere. She walked in silently and on the table placed something she came with. Then she returned to the door and peeped out, looking right and left. She groped in the darkness with her hands for the broken door panel and when she touched it she lifted it into position and returned to Okolo.

'Your match, where is it?' she asked.

'On the table's top.'

She moved to the table and groped for the match. 'And the lamp?' she asked after she had found the match.

'On the table's top, too.'

Thereupon, she scratched the match and lighted the lamp. She then picked up a knife from the table and cut the rope tying Okolo's hands.

'What is the root of this?' Okolo asked rubbing his wrists. Tuere did not open her mouth. She went to the table and untied what she had placed on the table. It was a covered enamel bowl and opening it, she pushed it towards Okolo with not a smile opening her mouth.

The smell of newly cooked yam and fresh fish made hunger hold him suddenly. No food had passed 'own his throat since yesterday but he had not felt hunger holding him until this standing moment. He lifted his right hand to the edge of the bowl but dropped it back. When she saw this, Tuere went to the water pot at the corner of the room but she found no water in it.

'I'll go and get water from the waterside,' she said and taking an empty bucket near the pot, moved quickly towards the door. Before Okolo could open his mouth to stop her, she had removed the door panel aside and had slipped out into the darkness. He ran to the door but she had gone and so he returned to the table and sat looking at the food. He sat thus smelling the smell of the yam and fish in the pepper soup. For one year it seemed to him, he waited, with hunger tightening its grip on him.

And when he lifted his hand and was about to touch the yam, he heard a small noise behind him. He dropped his hand guiltily. Tuere had returned and she had been away for only about five minutes.

Tuere put the bucket of water down, took a dish near the pot and poured in water. She held the dish of water out for Okolo and he washed his hands.

'Why are you doing all this for me?' Okolo asked after he had finished eating and had washed his hands.

Tuere sat twiddling her fingers as if Okolo's questioning words had not entered her ears. She sat twiddling her fingers.

'My inside has become hard, filled with thoughts as hard as stones,' she said suddenly, raising her head and looking straight at Okolo. 'I have from my inside thrown out all soft thoughts which women usually have towards men. All that is gone but my inside is sweet, the sweetness you get from getting what you want. This sweetness has increased since you came.'

She paused. Okolo looked at the lamp.

'I know these are not answering words to your questioning words but I do want you to really know me and the root of my actions which I think has made wonder hold you.' She again paused and made herself more comfortable on the chair.

Okolo gazed at the lamp.

'I have killed many moons, many years in that hut thinking of the happening things in this town. My feet know not the door of a school but Woyengi who all things created gave each of us human beings an inside and a head to think. So the many years I have killed in the hut have put many things into my inside which have made me see differently. To speak the straight thing, I was beginning to see things as if through a harmattan fog when they called me a witch and I was put out of the way by the Elders like a tree that has fallen across a path. I put a strong fear into their insides because they thought I was going to turn the insides of the people against them. So they got rid of me and felt they held the whole world in their hands until you came. At first they did not smell any danger. Why should they smell any danger? Was Abadi not there?

'Let my eyes be blind, as they are to your books, instead of going to school and coming out with a head and an inside like those he has. Yes, Abadi who has finished going to all big schools in this world did the same thing and had the same shallow inside that has

v.   33   B

room for nothing else but money and women. They did not see it in their insides that you could call a white thing white and not black since you've never been outside the country. That was what they saw in their insides and even acted on some of your suggestions.

'The people heard of your activities and all raised their hands for you. But Chief Izongo saw in this a personal challenge to himself.'

'How could this have put fear into Chief Izongo's inside?' asked Okolo naïvely after clearing his throat.

'You speak like a child,' said Tuere with her eyes softening. 'You are indeed a child in your inside. Don't you see it in your inside that when everybody raises his hand for you and sings your praise in song, you are turning the insides of the people against them? So you were a big tree fallen across their path. They could not move it or cut it as they did me because you have been to school. And so they had to cut a path around it by passing the word round that your head is not correct.'

She paused and looked at Okolo. Okolo also looked at her. They looked at one another. Then Okolo removed his eyes and looked behind her into the shadow.

'Wonder is holding you as you are thinking of how I, a woman who has not passed the doors of a school, know all this. Well, I have a head though I have not entered the doors of a school house, and having an open inside makes one know many things.'

Then she again started to talk when Okolo did not open his mouth to say anything.

'Chief Izongo and the Elders have very simple insides like the insides of children, in spite of what they say of themselves. One can read their insides as you read your books. They do these things in an open manner thinking that nobody knows or thinking nobody can stand in their path . . .'

She gathered the folds of her loin cloth tightly round her knees and sat back in the chair and again looked at

Okolo. Okolo yawned.

'You asked me why I am giving you my hands in this happening-thing, when you have become the enemy of everything in the town? Well, I am giving you my hands and my inside and even my shadow to let them see in their insides that if even the people do not know, we, you and I, know and have prepared our bodies to stand in front of them and tell them so. They now feel that I really am a witch, so I put fear into their insides. That sweetened my inside because I had wanted to remain a witch in their eyes so that I could do something against them. Then you returned, and when I started to hear the happening-things in your name, my hopes rose to the eye of the sky. And then yesterday you came running, being pursued by the people. So I called you in. These are my answering words to your questioning words.'

Tuere looked at Okolo. He was sleeping with his head on his chest. Her eyes became soft, in spite of herself. She rose from the chair, took her enamel bowl and tied it back in her faded headkerchief. She stood looking down at him and laying her hand on his shoulders shook him gently and pushed him down on the bed. Okolo turned on his side without opening his eyes and continued to sleep.

Okolo opened his eyes slowly lying on his back. As he opened his eyes slowly he heard the sounds of the morning coming to him from the outside. He shut his eyes again as he listened lying on his back. A new sound suddenly entered his ears. He opened his eyes and looked. He saw feet shuffling towards him. He raised his eyes from the feet and he saw his friends Benitu and Tudou, Chief Izongo's messengers. They stopped near the bed. Okolo looked at them. They looked at Okolo. Okolo looked at them, but he saw in their eyes not arrogance or hatred as before but pity and pain. He turned this over in his inside and again looked at them. They stood there without their mouths opening. They stood there shifting their weights from one foot to the

35

other and making wry faces like people taking nivaquine.

Benitu who appeared to be the leader made as if to
speak but nothing came out of his mouth. Then he
glanced at Tudou, urging with his eyes.

Okolo turned over this unusual behaviour of his
friends in his inside and saw that before him were
people who had thrown away their heads for Izongo's
patronage. The pity he felt for them touched his bones.
He was sure they were about to say something they were
finding hard to say because it would leave a lump of
nivaquine-bitterness in their insides. What could that be?

'What is it you want to say?' Okolo asked gently.

'It's Izongo,' Tudou succeeded in saying in a half
whisper.

'What about him?'

Tudou cleared his throat and cast a quick glance at
his companion. 'He says tomorrow is Sologa mail,' he
said, with his voice scarcely above a whisper.

'I know,' Okolo said, his inside sinking a little into
his voice. 'I would have left without his reminding me.'

THREE

The outboard engine-canoe laboured against the strong water of the river. It was rain's time. So the river was full up to its brim and the water's power passed power. So the outboard engine's sound was like the sound of an aeroplane as it pushed the canoe against the formidable power of the water. Slowly, slowly the canoe moved like the walk of an old man.

Okolo opened his eyes and looked in front of him. The people were sleeping. He looked towards his left. The people were sleeping. He looked towards his right. The people were sleeping. A man was snoring, and saliva flowing like an okra soup out of his mouth's corner. A woman, wearing an accra suit, though sleeping, held firmly her playing child sitting astride her lap. She was going to Sologa to meet her husband. A fat man with a belly like an oil puncheon, was breathing like a man blowing a fire, with his mouth open wide. He wore a dark singlet reaching down to only his navel and the sides were bursting. His boasting gone, by sleep taken. He was a whiteman's cook, so he said. He had told everybody loudly that he had, with his cooking, sent his son to college. His son would soon finish and join the Council and then money 'like water flow' he had said, rubbing his hands, and laughed a laugh which made the groaning engine sound like the feeble buzz of a mosquito. Okolo at the rising, falling, rising, falling cheeks, looked. They were rising, falling, rising, falling like the cheeks of a croaking frog. He was returning to Sologa from leave to meet his master. Okolo thus remembered the whiteman's cook's spoken-out words.

And next to Okolo on his left hand side, a girl sat. She rested her head on his shoulder, sleeping. She must have killed sixteen years. If not, she must have less or little more years killed. But she had reached a woman. Her breasts were standing and were not fallen. They were standing and were calabash breasts. She was dressed in an accra suit. A new one. Okolo had not heard a word coming out of her mouth, even when she had not slept. Silence, she was, itself. No, she was silent more than silence. She rested her head on Okolo's shoulder, sleeping. Next to her a woman sat, sleeping. She was sleeping and yet talking. Okolo looked at her. She must have killed forty to fifty years, for her hair was dark-brown instead of black. She must have dyed her hair which was now fading. But she was sleeping and yet talking. Okolo looked at her. Then she coughed and opened her eyes. Okolo quickly removed his eyes. Then he remembered her loudly spoken words which had come out of her mouth and had sped like bullets straight to the whiteman-food-cooker. She had with her deep masculine voice torn to pieces the engine's sound saying her son having passed standard six the previous year was now a clerk. A heap of money he was earning and the girl was his wife. No, they did not know each other but the girl had seen her son's photograph and liked him. And her son? Her son must like the girl for she had carefully chosen her out of many. She it was who had paid for her son's training and for this job paid twenty pounds and for his wife thirty pounds. Her son to whatever she said must listen and her inside told her he would like the girl.

Okolo thus remembered the spoken words that from the woman's mouth had come out like bullets straight to the whiteman's cook. And next to the whiteman's cook sat sleeping the man with the saliva flowing from his mouth's side. He seemed not to have tired of talking, recounting Sologa life – women and what not. But now he was sleeping like one who is sleeping death's sleep. He was indeed sleeping death's sleep. Okolo this man's spoken words stirred in his inside. In his inside he stirred them and looked. This man had said he had taken home bags of money and was now returning to Sologa. He was a policeman and to him on earth it was the best work, especially if one has a lucky head. If you have a lucky head and if you catch a rich trader stealing from a big whiteman's shop then on heaps of money you stand up to your knees. Why take a man like that to the station when stealing from a whiteman's shop? Whiteman takes all our money to his country.

Thus Okolo remembered the spoken words that from this policeman's mouth came out. Then opposite him sat a black-coat-wearing man with his head nodding, nodding. No, a black coat it was no longer. The sleeves were bag like, brown and frayed. And the neck shiny with his body sweat and grease. Okolo at the nodding, nodding head looked and the man's spoken words stirred in his inside. This man his suffering had bewailed, Okolo remembered. He said he lost his job because he had no one to stand in his front to speak for him, and no one to put hand for him to give the headman the twenty pounds he had asked. How could he the twenty pounds give, when he had not twenty pence? His month's pay was only six pounds and he had a wife and three children to feed and buy clothes for. So he came home to taste politics. And he had himself in politics mixed and stood for election. He was succeeding but only his rivals had money to give and he had not. So he failed. He was now returning to taste Sologa and see.

Thus this black-coat-wearing man his story had told and thus Okolo remembered.

The engine canoe against the strong water pushed and slowly, slowly it walked along the wide river with the tall iroko trees, kapok trees, palm trees, standing on its banks, the sky's eye reaching. Soon, the day's eye became bad. It became so bad and black and closed that it could not be looked at. And soon lightning flashed in the day's eye and the thunder sounded like the sound of one hundred cannons going off near your ears. All the passengers woke up with a shout. Thunder had torn their sleep and deafened their ears. Then they feared and shouted and spoke, not hearing each other.

'Stop the engine, stop the engine!' shouted the canoe steerer.

'Take the canoe to the ground, take the canoe to the ground!' the engineer shouted at the canoe steerer, their words knocking each other out into the wind and blowing away.

'Ee, Woyengi, sorry for us!'

'Things of the soil of the town, for today only save us!'

'How is it! How is it! Amadasu will you see us die?'

'Blow it away, blow it open!'

'Things that follow me! This about-to-happening big thing take away!'

'Kolokumo Egbesu! How?'

'O God deliver us! O, Christ, sorry for us, O.'

As everybody so prayed and invoked according to his or her religion, the forty to fifty years killed woman from her seat rose with eyes opened wide and like a man over the mass of legs, walked, stumbled, walked, stumbled, to the pointed canoe's bow. At the bow, straight she stood and her hands raised and eyes at the sky's eye-blackened river gazed. Thus for awhile she stood, her clothes billowing at her back like a sail. Then her man's voice she raised until the hard wind it pierced, invoking Benikurukuru, her clan's deity.

'Benikurukuru! Benikurukuru! How? Have you come to take me? How! Have I in something defaulted? A sign show. He-who-owns-us, a sign show. Show. . . . A sign show. Anything you ask I will sacrifice. Only show. . . .'

Then the sky suddenly broke and when the rain from above poured, it passed telling. The rain drops were like six-inch cannon balls. It did not rain like rain. It rained more than raining.

'Will you in the river take me? A sign show. Blow,

40

blow, the sky's eye blow open. . . .'

The roof was made of mats and it began to leak. It leaked and the rain water on the people's heads, backs, faces, hands, feet and noses fell, and their clothes started soaking through to the warm skins. The woman with the child had an umbrella. She opened it above her head and covered her child. The two men at her side, shoved their heads under it. Others who had nothing, covered their heads with clothes. But they were soon wet and they removed them.

Okolo had an old raincoat. He stood up and put it over his head and back and sat. It was old and had holes but it stood rain more than ordinary cloth. The people pressed each other for warmth. The girl who was going to her husband pressed on Okolo. All her body was almost wet. Okolo looked at her. She had no cover. He again stood up and with his elbows he opened out the raincoat to cover the girl and sat. The girl from her waist up faced Okolo, hesitated and then on him pressed closer to make the raincoat cover all her body. When the girl's wet clothes his body touched Okolo shivered. The girl quickly uncovered herself and quickly removed her sticking blouse and then resumed her former position. And her husband's mother not looking at the big rain, not looking at the wind, not looking at her clothes sticking to her body, and not looking at the hurrying waves, waves hurrying with white caps as if to deliver a message, she stood like a sail post fixed to the bow, invoking her clan god.

'Today only, today only, forgive me. . . . O, one with black face. Today only. . . .'

And Okolo sitting with the girl pressed on him under the raincoat covering them, talked to his inside.

'Protect her . . . she is a male person, she is a male person, a male person, male person, male person, male person. . . . Protect her. She knows nothing. A male person. . . .'

'Today only . . . today only. . . .'

41

Soon, the wind abated and finally stopped. The rain also little by little stopped. Then the waves disappeared and the thunder rumbled away into the heavens and the day's eye opened and the sun appeared.

'Today you have shown again. You have shown,' shouted the woman in ecstasy. 'Guard me safely to Sologa and back home safely guard me. I will make sacrifice. I vow!'

Then she lowered her hands slowly to her sides and her loin cloth gathered up to her thighs and the water squeezed out. Then she removed her blouse over her head and squeezing out the water, spread it on the canoe's roof. And then she called her son's wife to bring her from her box, another loin cloth and blouse. Okolo shook the girl sleeping on his lap.

'Ebiere, Ebiere,' the call came from the bow. 'Is she sleeping?'

'He is shaking her,' someone said.

Then she bent and peeped into the canoe and with a strong voice called. Then she saw the girl emerging from Okolo's raincoat. She withdrew her head quickly and struck her palms together in alarm.

'Apo! Apo! Apo!' she shouted, striking her palms together in rhythm. 'On a man's lap sleeping! Apo! Apo! Apo!'

As she thus shouted, some male passengers looked at Okolo and laughed. Okolo, too, looked at them and entered the laughter and laughed. And in the girl's eyes sleep had now been torn away and in wonder she look at the men laughing. The men laughed more and more. As she in wonder looked, she heard her husband's mother shouting and lowered her eyes.

'Apo! Apo! Apo! So it's true, so it's true. So what they say it's true! That's how they tempt for themselves the women going to their husbands' places. I believed not before. Apo! Apo! Apo!' Thus she shouted, spoke and shouted and struck her palms together in rhythm. And inside the canoe, the puncheon-belly-owning man, the whiteman's cook yawned, and chuckling said : 'Is she not beautiful?' He again chuckled.

The laughter that Okolo was laughing immediately left his lips.

'I did something, you think?' he thus asked the whiteman's cook.

And the whiteman's cook laughing said, 'This thing nobody ever agrees to this thing.'

Okolo now knew the heavy thing they wanted to put on his head. He looked at the girl. She had shifted away and was squeezing her cloth. And the men looked at them and laughed.

'You are a bad girl,' one of the women passengers said. 'You are just a small fish doing this sort of thing. Girls of today are not like girls of yesterday.'

'All of you my witnesses be,' said the mother-in-law tearing her way into the canoe to Okolo's front.

'And you this man, between you and me a big thing has fallen. Not one word from your mouth has come out since you joined the canoe. You have been silent more than silence. So in your silence you were knotting bad thoughts in your inside. This big thing will not finish here. All of you my witnesses be. You all saw how my son's wife was on his lap covered with raincoat. Did he anything to you do?' she the girl asked. 'Did he no part of your body touch?'

The girl her head shook.

'It's a lie! The truth speak. If you the truth speak not, things of the ground will hold you.'

'You, this woman, listen to me,' Okolo strongly spoke. 'I did nothing to her. Her clothes all were wet and cold and she shivering sat and so I only spread my raincoat and covered her and she slept. And all the time she slept, in my inside, a boy I took her. I, in the way you think, did not touch her,' he ended naïvely.

'Any man who does such a thing always has a strong mouth,' said a man.

'Kpe! kpe! kpe! let me laugh,' said the mother-in-law

and sat on her former place and then suddenly got up and sat between Okolo and the girl.

'You say you want to find a woman? Now find me,' said she.

'For what reason are you people putting fire to this thing?' Okolo, the whiteman's cook and the other man asked quietly.

'You know not?' asked the whiteman's cook.

'Because the girl does not speak, he has a strong mouth.'

'He has no shame,' said the mother-in-law.

'What thing ought I to know?' Okolo asked the whiteman's cook, the mother-in-law's words as nothing taking. 'Have I done anything to you? I do not know you.'

'Even if a person inside water lets out gas, the odour floats up to the surface. You know not even this the saying of our Izon people?'

Okolo looked at his palms. The whiteman's cook chuckled.

'So he has this thing done before?' asked a woman with a fear-and-surprise-mixed voice.

'You cannot a thing I have done not put on my head.' Thus strongly Okolo spoke. 'How can you on my head put a thing that happened not? It is true I have spoken not to anyone since the canoe I entered. That was because my inside if filled with forcing thoughts up to my throat which I dare speak not. . . .'

'This is a lying story. You know not this man,' jumped in the whiteman's cook. 'You know not this man. His mouth is very very sweet. Listen not to him. News is like a wind. I know him.'

'You, that man, why allow him not to speak,' the engine man the whiteman's cook addressed. 'This woman is putting a happened-or-not thing on his head. Let us hear him. I do not like how you his mouth want to close.'

The whiteman's cook rolled round, his breath in quick gusts coming out of his mouth as if he was blow-

ing a fire. His eyes turned red like a red paint and his
face became so hard it could dent the sharp edge of a
matchet. He looked at the engine man as if to look him
to death. And his mouth opened and shut, opened and
shut, opened and shut like a fowl, a bigger-than-throat
thing swallowing. Then the voice itself squeezed out of
his throat sounding like corn exploding on fire.

'You, you, you small fish-egg boy speaking to me
like this? The whiteman, my father, even like this
spoke not to me. Who are you? A son like you I have
in college. You, look, do not put your mouth in this
matter.'

'Because a son you have in college nobody will speak
the straight thing?' the engine man said. 'I too have a
brother in college.'

'Ta! your mouth shut,' the whiteman's cook wheezed
out, his breath ssh-ssh-ssh like a railway engine in high
speed sounding. 'You your body take care, your body
take care. . . .'

'What can you do?' the engine man said haughtily.
And when he this heard the whiteman's cook's inside
boiled and stank more than any odour that if it were
dropped into the river the fishes would die, and if it
were to be smelled, the people in the canoe would have
been suffocated. He tried to heave himself up but his
inside stopped him.

'What can you do, you who only cook whiteman's
food?' taunted the engineer. 'You have been cooking
whiteman's food until your body has become a jelly
fish and your head has flown away in the smoke. What do
you know?'

As the whiteman's cook with one supreme effort
and a big grunt heaved himself up, the canoe to the
other side listed and the people in fear and dismay,
shouted. With a big bump, he dropped back on his
seat, but the canoe again on his side listed heavily. The
people knowing well a canoe's behaviour moved not
and from side to side it swayed until it righted itself.

When the canoe had settled evenly on the water, the mother-in-law, without moving from her seat, took a soft soft voice to beg the engine man and the white-man's cook.

'Say nothing more on this matter. This wanted-to-happen thing, on my head it should have fallen. The rain and storm they came and passed away because I the god begged. And this nearly ourselves lost in water. It is my bad head. Talk no more of my son's wife, talk no more, of this matter, talk no more.'

'It's that small fish-egg boy,' breathed the whiteman's cook.

'Do not call me a small fish-egg boy,' the engine man said warningly.

'Why did you a bad man's side enter?' the white-man's cook's supporter asked the engine man. Before the engine man his mouth opened to answer, the woman who had called the girl a bad girl said:

'You know not? If you a bird of the sky take and in front of a fowl roast, the fowl's head aches.'

'You mean me?' asked the engine man of the woman.

'I mentioned nobody's name. I only put a parable.'

'You hear something of me?'

'Stop now, please, please,' pleaded the mother-in-law.

'No, I will not stop. She must mention the hidden thing I have done.'

'You do not know yourself?' said the woman and smiled a little.

'Ah, so I have done something that you know? Say it, say it. If you do not say it, this canoe will not move. This canoe moves not if you say not. You do not know me yet,' said the engine man at the woman shouting and gesticulating.

At this, all the other passengers, the whiteman's cook and his supporter, excepting, turned their mouths on the woman.

'Why did you talk on a finished matter?' a man of the woman demanded.

'You women from Sologa talk too much,' said another.

'The matter touched you not at all. Now you have the engine man's inside made to boil. If we here stop, it will on your head fall.'

As all the passengers the woman so blamed, the whiteman's cook breathing, whoosh, whoosh, whoosh and with his cheeks rising and falling, rising and falling, looked at this face and looked at that face.

'Listen not to her,' said another, the engine man begging.

'I agree not,' said he. 'I agree not. If she any bad thing of me knows, let her say, if not, this canoe moves not. Let her say, if not, let her and myself by any god swear.'

'My man, open your ears and listen to me,' Okolo addressed the engine man. 'Listen to me, my man. You only entered my side, so I thank you. This thanks that I am thanking you comes from my inside. So I will with all my inside speak some teaching words to you. This world is very big. To every person's said-thing listen not. If you listen to every said-thing in this world, you cannot achieve anything or you the wrong thing will do. If your inside says this is a straight thing, do it. Let not people's said-things your inside spoil. So, to this woman's said-thing, listen not. Your ears close. Here many there are who have said nothing and if this canoe does not leave this place they will have suffering on their heads for nothing. So I am begging you, listen not to her.'

The engine man Okolo's said-things heard and started the engine and the canoe once more, like an old man up a slope walking, moved slowly forward until making-people-handsome day appeared. Then the sun went down the tree tops and night from the river rose and shrouded the river sides and then the tree tops in shadows, and closed the eye of the sky. In this darkness the canoe moved, groping, moved with Okolo in his inside turning thoughts over and over.

47

FOUR

Okolo's leaving town was Izongo's rejoicing. His inside
was sweeter than sweetness and he was with the spirit
of kindness possessed (so he told his Elders) and so he
gathered all the people of Amatu : men, women, children, the lame, the deaf and dumb and the blind. All
the people came hurrying to Izongo's compound. Even
the deaf and dumb looking at lips as a hungry person
looks at the mouths of people eating, hurried; and the
blind, staring hard at nothing, guided by stamping
feet and voices, groped; and the lame with dust in their
eyes from heels that looked at nothing, crawled to
Izongo's compound.

When the people : men, women, children, the lame,
the deaf and dumb and the blind had gathered in his
compound, Izongo stood up from his raised seat at the
centre and spoke.

'Men, women and children of Amatu. Today is a
great day. Look at the eye of the day. This is rain's time
but the eye of the day is cleaner than cleanliness even
though the sound of the rain in the three days past
has been like that of a stream falling on rocks. Yet
today the eye of the sky suddenly opened and the wind
has blown the rain to the south. What is the root of
this? The root of this is that yesterday I and the Elders
swept from this town a stinking thing. (Here there was a
great applause.) A stinking thing like a rotten corpse
be, which had made us all, you and me, breathe freely
no more for the many years past. Now we are free
people be, free to breathe.

'It was a great task I performed, my people. A great
task in sending him away. A dangerous task, but it
had to be done for the good of us all. We did it with
our eyes on our occiputs, for it is a strong thing be to

48

send away one who is looking for it. Only a madman looks for *it* in this turned world. Let him look for *it* in this wide world if he can find *it*. But we don't want him to stay here asking, "Have you *it*? Have you *it*? Have you *it*?" Even in our sleep we hear him asking. We know not what *it* is. We do not want to know. Let us be as we are. We do not want to be troubled by one whose inside is filled with water. So, let us be.'

Izongo paused and surveyed the crowd : the men, women, children, the deaf, the dumb, the blind, the crippled, the lame of Amatu, shuffling their feet under his gaze. He looked from face to face and continued :

'Only one small thing more before we drink palm-wine. Only one small thing more. It's a very soft thing, soft as water, softer than softness. What I will say is a questioning word and you will answer in one answering word. Now open your ears and listen. I and the Elders have here decided not to allow Okolo to come back to this our town. If he shows his face in this town we shall send him, and any person like him, away for ever and ever. Do you to this agree?'

Loud shouts of 'Yes! Yes!' came out from the throat of Amatu, led by the Elders. Shouts of 'Yes! Yes!' drowned Okolo's lone voice asking, 'Is *it* here? Have you *it*? Is *it* here?' for ever they thought, in their insides.

Then, with smile smile, Izongo looked at the people and with a wave of the hand, the palmwine ordered around. And the people rejoiced, their insides like honey becoming, and drank and drank.

As the people drank and drank, a cripple who was at the rear, looking and listening between legs that looked at nothing, crawled quietly away. He crawled away as if making for his own house. But when he reached his house he did not stop. He crawled past it and made for the edge of the forest where stood Tuere's hut. And when he reached Tuere's hut the door opened and in he crawled. In he crawled to the darkness of the room with the living flame in the hearth, a living flame creating

Tuere's shadow on the wall.

'I hear them singing,' said Tuere.

'Yes,' the cripple said, 'yes, they are singing with voices like a piece of earth, and drinking with throats that pick nothing, and shaking the world with their looking-at-nothing feet.'

'What is the bottom of this?' Tuere asked.

'Izongo in this town wants him no more. If he shows his face in this town again, he and anyone like him will be sent away for ever and ever.'

'For ever and ever,' she whispered, then aloud, 'Why do they want to do this bad thing to him who has done nothing bad to them? Why? Why? Why? O, why?' she grieved.

'Tell him to search for *it* no more,' advised the cripple.

'He will not stop. He asked it of Woyengi. Nobody can stop him. No, I will not ask him to stop.'

'Then tell him to come back no more.'

'No, his umbilical cord is in the ground of this town buried. So he will come back.'

'To be sent away for ever and ever?'

'To the call of the umbilical cord everybody answers "yes" wherever one may be, you know that.'

'I know, but anyone like him will be sent away too.'

'Yes. I fear not. It's they, the world, who fear.'

'But the world has turned.'

'Yes, the world has turned, and the people's insides are owned by fear.'

'So he will come back? And you too will go with him?'

'If it's what I asked of Woyengi, it will so happen.'

'May we live to see tomorrow,' the cripple said as he moved to the door.

The cripple went out into the darkness and Tuere let the mat fall slowly over the door. She then turned and sat by the hearth with the living flame creating her shadow on the wall.

FIVE

Okolo his dead legs stretched as the canoe slid aground on the shores of Sologa. He gripped his small box as passengers began moving. Then bending double, the roof being too low, Okolo, too, made his way slowly to the canoe's bow and stepped down on the soil of Sologa of Seitu, the Big One.

As Okolo stood on the soil of Sologa trying to pierce the thickness of the night with his eyes, a voice close to his ears startled him with a whisper.

'I have not the big thing between us forgotten. You will of my doings hear concerning it.'

Before Okolo recovered from this the shadowy figure of a woman gripping a girl by the hand slid into the night, a black night like the back of a cooking pot. As Okolo gazed at the spot where the woman and the girl had with the night merged like a drop of water into a river, he was again startled by a voice close to him.

'Are you Okolo?' the voice was asking.

'Yes. Who are you?' Okolo asked in surprise.

'We were sent to meet you.'

'To meet me? Who sent you? I know no one in Sologa.'

'Do not try to know the bottom of things.'

'Isn't it a mistake you are making? Are you not taking me for someone else?'

The voice chuckled and said : 'We are taking you to a place where you can find *it*.' At this two chunks of darkness detached themselves from the darkness and gripped Okolo's hands and pushed him through the black black night like the back of a cooking pot.

Through the black black night Okolo walked, stumbled, walked. His inside was a room with chairs, cushions, papers scattered all over the floor by thieves. Okolo walked, stumbled, walked. His eyes shut and opened, shut and opened, expecting to see a light in each opening, but none he saw in the black black night.

At last the black black night like the back of a cooking pot entered his inside and grabbing his thoughts, threw them out into the blacker than black night. And Okolo walked, stumbled, walked with an inside empty of thoughts except the black black night.

When Okolo came to know himself, he was lying on a floor, on a cold cold floor lying. He opened his eyes to see but nothing he saw, nothing he saw. For the darkness was evil darkness and the outside night was black black night. Okolo lay still in the darkness enclosed by darkness, and he his thoughts picked in his inside. Then his picked thoughts his eyes opened but his vision only met a rock-like darkness. The picked thoughts then drew his legs but his legs did not come. They were as heavy as a cone full of sand. His thoughts in his inside began to fly in his inside darkness like frightened birds, thither, homeless. . . . Then the flying thoughts drew his hand but the hands did not belong to him, it seemed. So Okolo on the cold cold floor lay with his body as soft as an over-pounded foo foo. So Okolo lay with his eyes open wide in the rock-like darkness staring, staring.

Okolo for years and years lay on the cold cold floor at the rock-like darkness staring. Then suddenly he saw a light. He drew his feet with all his soul and his feet came. He drew his hands and his hands came. He stood up with his eyes on the light and walked towards the light. As he moved towards the light the light also moved back. He moved faster and the light also moved faster back. Okolo ran and the light also ran. Okolo ran, the light ran. Okolo ran and hit a wall with his head. Okolo looked and the light was no more. He then stretched his hands forth and touched the wall. His fingers felt dents and holes. Okolo walked sideways like a crab with his fingers on the wall, feeling dents and holes, dents and holes in the rock-like darkness until his feet struck an object. As Okolo stopped and felt the object his body became cold. His heartbeat echoed in the rock-like darkness and his head expanded. Still, he felt along the object until his fingers went into two holes. As his fingers went into the holes he quickly withdrew them and ran. He ran and fell, ran and fell over other objects. He ran and knocked again the wall and fell. Still he ran, then suddenly stopped. He saw a light in front of him. He moved gently crouching forward like a hunter stalking game. Then when he nearly reached the light, he rushed forward.

Okolo found himself standing in daylight in a street, hither and thither turning his eyes. He stood turning his eyes this way and that way in the street. Thus he stood with the crowd passing him by: cars honking, people shouting, people dying, women delivering, beggars begging for alms, people feasting, people crying, people laughing, politicians with grins that do not reach their insides begging for votes, priests building houses, people doubting, people marrying, people divorcing, priests turning away worshippers, people hoping, hopes breaking platelike on cement floors. Thus Okolo stood watching the crowd pass him by until he saw a constable approaching with eyes that nothing saw and feet that did not touch the ground. Okolo went to him and talked to him. As Okolo talked to him, down went the constable's eyebrows to his nose and up they went again into the peak of his cap. Then his mouth hardened stonelike. And when Okolo finished his story, he broke into a grin, a comforting grin and brought out his notebook.

'This thing you say is a big thing,' the constable said, and brought out his pencil, a short pencil with many many teeth marks. 'But the owner of the house you mention is also a big man,' he again said, adjusting his belt. 'To which tribe you belong?' he asked Okolo.

'Tribe does not come into this,' Okolo said with small temper.

'You a new man be in Sologa?' asked the constable unperturbed.

'Yes, only yesterday I reached here.'

'Oho, you are a new man be, and what is your business?'

'I reached here only yesterday-yesterday, Thursday, the 15th day of July, and into the house I was taken.'

At this the constable frowned, pointed his lips, brought his diary out and with his stubby finger checked the dates. When he had checked the dates he asked Okolo to follow him. He stopped at a street corner.

'We can now talk here without being disturbed,' he said in an undertone. 'I am a law man be but what you say of the big man is so big I must accurately take it down. You say you reached here yesterday?'

'Yes,' Okolo answered. 'I reached here yesterday'

'And people dragged you away?'

'Yes, people dragged me away and put me in the dark room with bones like. . . .'

'Not so fast. People dragged you away and put you in the dark room. Yes?'

'With bones like human. . . .'

'Ssh! This is not a true thing. So do not say it. People will believe not. Did you with your eyes see the bones?'

'No, I felt one.'

'Aha.'

'It's true!'

'Aha, it's true, but with your eyes you saw it? This man a big man be.'

'Let's go to the house and –'

'My Jesus! I have a family, man! – a wife and two children and one is in college. My Jesus, go to the big man's house and look for human bones? You are an intelligent man be.'

'The law looks at no one's face,' Okolo said.

'Oho, you are a new man be in Sologa.'

Then he whispered into Okolo's ear : 'The law looks at this big man's face. I tell you thus because you are an intelligent man be.'

'Then you will not investigate?' Okolo asked.

'No, no, no, no. I did not say that. I am a law man be, so I will now investigate. Wait for me here.'

With this the constable this way and that way looked and walked towards the direction of the house. And when he saw Okolo no more, entered a telephone booth. He brought out the piece of paper on which he had written Okolo's statement and putting it into his mouth, chewed it. Then he came out and went to a bar and washed it down with a beer!

Okolo waited and waited for the constable but the constable did not return. He stood there and waited with the crowd passing him by, but Okolo even the constable's shadow did not see. So to the inside of Sologa of the Big One he walked with each step begging the ground. So Okolo walked in Sologa of the Big One passing frustrated eyes, ground-looking eyes, harlots' eyes, nothing-looking eyes, hot eyes, cold eyes, bruised eyes, despairing eyes, nothing-caring eyes, grabbing eyes, dust-filled eyes, aping eyes. . . .

Okolo walked passing eyes, walked passing eyes, walked passing eyes until hunger held him. Then his eyes hither, thither looked for an eating house. But none he saw. So he walked forward. He continued to walk begging the ground until a man he saw standing by the street side and asked him where an eating house he could find. The man staring over Okolo's shoulder never a word said. Okolo went closer and asked again. Still no answer. So Okolo nicely looked at him.

Looking at something far away the man appeared to be with his ears listening, with his ears opened wide to catch every sound, every word spoken by the passing crowd. But Okolo's voice he heard not. After nicely looking at him, Okolo asked again explaining that he was a stranger man be in Sologa. But the man his mouth opened not. The man just stood there with perspiration running from his forehead to his eyes, nose and mouth. He did not even raise his hand to beat off a fly standing on his neck, washing its feet.

Okolo continued to walk begging the ground of Sologa of the Big One, alone in the passing crowds. Crowds of men, women, children talking, shouting wares, bananas, oranges, moimoi, akara. But he wanted an eating house and the hunger which held him dragged him forward until a man he met, a man smiling at him. Encouraged by the smile on the man's mouth. Okolo approached him and asked for directions.

'Are you a stranger man be?' the man asked.

'Yes,' Okolo said.

The man nodded, a knowing head. 'And you want an eating house?'

'Yes. I am very hungry,' Okolo confessed.

'But you are in front of an eating house and I am the owner.'

The man smiled as Okolo stood in surprise.

'Go inside and eat what you want,' he urged Okolo.

So inside Okolo went needing little urging. And as he entered he felt all eyes turned on him, for the eating and drinking and talking stopped.

'Eat and drink and talk in peace,' said he who owned the eating house as he by the side of Okolo stood. Everybody their eating and talking started.

'He is the expected one.'

As he who owned the eating house said this they stopped eating and laughed loud, some with food dropping from their mouths, others with drink going down the wrong side of their throats, choking, coughing, tears in their eyes appearing. The floor held Okolo's feet and he tried to run out. He who owned the eating house held him and into his ears spoke.

'All our insides and your inside are one. So fear not. Find a place and sit and I will bring you some food.'

56

'If what you say is a true thing be why they laugh thus?' Okolo asked.

'I will tell you,' promised he who owned the eating house. 'A place find for yourself and I will bring you food.'

With this he left Okolo and went into the kitchen, and Okolo found a place and sat. And the people looked at Okolo and then continued laughing as they their drinking continued and their eating continued. Wonder held Okolo to his seat. It was not long. He who owned the eating house came out from the kitchen with a plate of garri and another of soup balanced on his palms and placed them on Okolo's table. Then he brought water for washing hands and Okolo washed his hands and started eating. As Okolo ate the people drinking palmwine, beer and burukutu; laughed. They laughed and drank. Okolo ate urged by hunger. They laughed. Okolo ate. They laughed. Okolo ate until he finished his eating and washed his hands and his breathing reached the ground. His breathing reached the ground, and as he looked round the room at the people, he saw him who owned the eating house draw a curtain open at the back wall of the house.

There were things written in black across the white wall. Okolo read. 'Even the whiteman's Jesus failed to make the world fine. So let the spoilt world spoil.' Then below this, written in bolder letters was : 'Eat and drink O, die one day we go.' And further below this was yet another inscription in equally bold letters, which read thus : 'If we die tomorrow Mammy water go bury we.' As Okolo read these written things on the wall, he who owned the eating house came and sat near Okolo with smile in his mouth. 'They are our slogans be,' said he.

Okolo opened not his mouth. He sat quiet like cold water. He who owned the house with smile smile drew his chair closer and said : 'Have a sweet inside, my friend, and be merry and without fearing speak.' Then

Okolo without fearing spoke and asked who the men were who in the street stood looking at no one but looking at everyone like portraits hanging on a wall. Whereupon he who owned the eating house laughed.

'They are the listeners of the Big One,' he said when he had finished laughing, and asked Okolo not to go any further in his search. But Okolo only shook his head. Thereupon he who owned the eating house spoke sound teaching words: 'Look, my man, stay here with us. This thing you are searching you cannot find here. You can only this thing find in rubbish heaps or in night soil dumps and those who go there do not come back. If they do, everybody will run away from them – the high and even the low – because of the stench. So to my teaching words listen and with us stay. We here, too, we have our best tried, but it is like trying to see if the body of a person who is in the water with you is dry.' He paused and waited for Okolo to speak, but Okolo opened not his mouth, so he continued his teaching words.

'So, my man, try not to see if I am dry. I am wet from my head to my feet and so are you. If you are not then your skin is duck's feathers but duck's feet get wet.' Okolo made as if to leave but again sat as he who owned the eating house started again to speak.

'The thing that is driving you is in your inside. You in your inside see the world like a tree on you falling and with your hands you want to hold it, knowing you will be crushed to death. Why die death that does not reach you? Do not think any more, my man. The people who have the sweetest insides are the think-nothing people and we here try to be like them. Like logs in the river we float and go whither the current commands and nothing enters our insides to turn the sweetness into bitterness. So, my man, here stay and be one of us.' But Okolo again only his head shook, thanked him and left with everybody at him staring.

So Okolo the eating house left and in the street stood looking this way and that way trying to decide which way to take. After standing thus for awhile with the people passing up and down he decided to follow the stream of people going to his left. He this choice made not because he believed it would lead him to his goal but he was a man standing at the water's edge of a cold river to bathe. In spite of the cold he has to jump in and have done with it. So Okolo thought in his inside and the left stream of people took.

Okolo followed the think-nothing stream and a part of the stream he became. His eyes caught a sign board proclaiming its owner's belief in the whiteman's God, the blackman's Gods, in front of a workshop. Okolo stopped and looked inside and in a corner he saw surrounded by heads a carver, creating heads out of created wood. With his missionary eyes seeing the face in the wood and with his moving lips he tapped at the chisel head and the falling off chips revealed a face. Okolo his inside turned as the carver tapped at his chisel. Okolo at the sign board looked and wondered what was behind it. To the carver Okolo turned his inside. It is to believe in everything or believe in nothing. The carver believes and puts even his shadow into creating faces out of wood and his inside is sweeter than sweetness. In what does he himself believe? Does he in what he is searching believe? Yes, he believes in *it*. *It* is there but his inside is not sweet. That is the difference. The sweetness of his inside is in finding *it*. . . . As Okolo stood there talking to himself in his inside a rough hand shook his shoulder from behind. Okolo, startled, turned and looking down on him were the unblinking eyes of one of the tall listeners of the Big One.

'You want to see the Big One?' said the listener with a caring-nothing voice. Okolo opened not his mouth for awhile and then said, 'Yes,' with a voice that said, 'I too, I am caring-nothing even death'.

'Come, I will take you to him.' With this the listener held Okolo's hand and walked towards the opposite direction in which Okolo had walked for many hours.

'Leave my hand. I will follow you to the Big One without your dragging me,' Okolo said as people stopped and looked at him. The listener heard him not. If he heard, Okolo's voice was like the ant that was crawling up the neck of one of his fellows. So Okolo followed without his mouth opening any more until the listener stopped at a door and with his left hand still gripping Okolo's hand, knocked. The listener then open cautiously and entered, dragging Okolo with him.

Sitting there behind a large table was a whiteman reading something in a file. On seeing the whiteman Okolo's inside became sweet. For here was someone who would understand what he was in search of and would certainly lead him to the Big One.

The listener stood there like a pole waiting to be seen. But the whiteman kept reading. The whiteman read, the listener stood. The whiteman read, the listener stood. Then at last the whiteman without his eyes raising said : 'Leave him and go.' Therefore the listener tiptoed out of the door and shut it gently.

The whiteman raised his eyes and looked at Okolo from head to foot. Then he rested his elbows on the table and clasped his hands in front of him.

'You speak English, of course?'

'Yes,' answered Okolo.

'You want to see the Big One?'

'Yes.'

'What about?'

'I want to ask him if he's got *it*.'

'Have you ever heard of the word psychiatrist?'

'Yes.'

'Do you know what a psychiatrist does?'

'Yes.'

'Have you consulted one?'

'No.'

'Why not?'

'Because I do not need his services.'

'I think you need the services of one badly.'

'Why?'

'Because I think you are going mental.'

'Going mental?' Okolo repeated slowly.

'Yes, you are going mental.'

'Why do you think I am going mental? Is it because I am searching for *it*? I thought you would understand,' Okolo said almost pleadingly.

'I am just trying to be helpful.'

'Trying to be helpful? You can only be helpful by taking me to the Big One.'

'That, my lad, I cannot and will not do. My instructions are that you are to be taken to the asylum. You are not wanted here. You have given too much trouble already in Sologa. You are to be confined here in a room until you are taken to the asylum.'

'But, but, I've given no one any trouble. You know that.'

'My dear lad, I've got a job to do and I will do it, see?' he said drumming on the table with his fingers.

'Even when you know it's wrong?'

'Don't ask me. This is your country. Ask your people.'

'Then take me to the Big One. He's one of my people.'

'I see, you are one of those smart alecs,' the whiteman said petulantly as he got up from his chair. 'You wait until we move out and see what will happen to men like you.' The whiteman, he, then, moved round and walked to the window. He, then, leaning on the window, looked outside, looked and looked singing a song with no words, no tune, tapping the floor with his shoe. He, then, moved from the window and walked to Okolo and put a hand on Okolo's shoulder.

'What I have just said is off the record,' he said with smile smile in his mouth. 'You forget what I said about what will happen to you when we move out of your country. You forget everything and I will make

61

things easy for you.'

'You mean you are going to let me see the Big One?'

'No, no, no. I do not mean that. I mean if you have your people here I'll ask them to come and take you.'

'I am not going to see the Big One?' Okolo said with the sweetness leaving him.

'Well, I am afraid so.'

'Why?'

'I've already told you. Be sensible and be a good lad. This country will need men like you, if only you learn to shut your eyes at certain things.'

'Then I won't be true to myself,' said Okolo.

'Look, my son, life isn't that way,' the whiteman started with a quiet teaching voice. 'Life's like playing checkers. If you make the wrong move you are finished. There are some to whom you can tell the truth, however unpleasant, about them to their faces and you get away with it. But the same won't be true of others. They may make things very, very unpleasant for you. See?'

'You don't believe in truth and honesty, then?'

'Look, my lad, these things simply don't exist in real life, if you want to get anywhere, if you want to make good. But mind you, I am not saying I do not believe in them. All I am saying is, you have to be judicious. No one will thank you, especially one who is in authority, for telling him by implication that you are, morally, a better person. You've got to be discreet. You just put on the act and "Open, Sesame!" As simple as that.'

Okolo spoke with his inside for awhile arguing the teaching of the whiteman. But no light he saw.

'All I want to do in my search,' Okolo spoke out at last, 'is to revitalize my flagging faith, faith, in man, belief in something,' he said with all his inside and his shadow. 'Belief and faith in that something we looked up to in times of sorrow and joy have all been taken away and in its stead what do we have? Nothing but a dried pool with only dead wood and skeleton leaves. And when you question they fear a tornado is going to blow down the beautiful houses they have built without foundations.'

Okolo talked and talked pouring out his inside and when it was at last exhausted he stopped. When he stopped he looked this way. There was nobody. He looked that way. There was nobody. He was standing alone. The whiteman had left him. He tried the door to open but it was locked. So he sat on a bench along one forbidding wall of the room and waited, speaking with his inside, thinking of the proverb of his people, the Ijaws, which says, 'If you roast a bird of the air before a fowl, the fowl's head aches'. So his inside many questions asked. Faith and faithlessness adding up to nothing. Belief and unbelief adding up to nothing. Man has no more shadow, trees have no more shadow. Nothing has any more meaning but the shadow-devouring trinity of gold, iron, concrete. . . Then he asked his inside what road to take in the immediate problem — to go back home, if that is possible, or go to the asylum.

One voice said he should to the asylum go. People whose heads are not correct perhaps have insides that are not sweet or bitter and he might learn to empty his own inside of sweetness and bitterness. Another voice said no, he should find a way to go back home. Chief Izongo and his Elders might have cleaned their insides of evil against him. The voice blamed him for leaving home. Don't people sweep the insides of their houses first before they sweep the outside? So the voice asked him and he agreed. Okolo agreed with the teaching words of the voice in his inside and decided to go back home and face Izongo. But the other voice said Chief Izongo and his Elders could not have changed in so short a time and that if he went back, Izongo's inside would become more septic and stink from earth to the eye of the sky. But these teaching words filed in through one of Okolo's ears and filed out through the other like canoes going one by one through a canal. So, in the end, Okolo said he must to his village return, if he could. But this time he would the masses ask and not Izongo and his Elders. If the masses haven't got *it*, he will create *it* in their insides. He will plant *it*, make *it* grow in spite of Izongo's destroying words. He will uproot the fear in their insides, kill the fear in their insides and plant *it*. He will all these do, if only . . . if only what? Okolo asked, speaking out, but his inside did not answer. And when he looked, he saw only darkness, the kind of darkness you see when you close your eyes at night.

SIX

In the village of Amatu, Chief Izongo rose one morning, the morning that made the seventh morning since from the town he drove Okolo, and spoke with his inside and agreed with his inside to celebrate his freedom from Okolo. So he agreed with his inside; but he also with his inside became free of the voice of Okolo like the voice of a mosquito which had driven even sleep out of their eyes. So Chief Izongo sent his messengers to the Elders who willingly or unwillingly had their insides put in his inside. Since Okolo left they had become more so and they heard each other on whatever that was decided. Indeed, they had become so close that even a torrent could not pass between them.

So two messengers set forth to deliver their errand.

'Why are you still with empty feet walking on this cold cold ground?' So asked one messenger of the other.

'On this cold cold ground we have been walking. Your money, what did you take to do?'

'Nothing I did with the money.'

'Nothing, why?'

'It is bad money. Bad money never brings good to anyone.'

'They are buying engine canoes with the money. Is that not good? My feet are not empty and this cold cold ground does not touch my feet any more. Is that not good? Your money, what did you take to do?'

'Nothing I take to do.'

'You are keeping it?'

'I do not know what I should take the money to do.'

Then they in silence walked, one walking with empty feet on the cold cold ground and the other with new black shoes.

'The spoken words of Okolo are entering your inside?'

'Do not ask me. In this thing I am with you.'

'This money, where is it?'

'What I do with money does not touch you. So do not ask.'

'I hear, but when Izongo asks what will you say?'

'What I take my money to do does not touch him.'

'Do not let water into your inside like Okolo. You want what happened to him to happen to you?'

'Sometimes my inside tells me it is not right.'

'What is not right?'

'What we did to him.'

Quickly pressing his hands against his ears his companion said : 'Your spoken words do not enter my ears. I am deaf. Speak no more of this.'

With this he walked faster, his hands still pressed against his ears. Soon he started to limp. Then he began walking like one with a dead foot. Then he stopped and bending down removed his shoes.

'Why your black black shoes remove?' asked the other with empty feet. Still bending and his toes examining, the black black shoe man did not open his mouth until he straightened up with the new black black shoes hanging from his left hand.

'My toes they squeezed too much,' he said softly softly.

'I say the money is bad money. Let this a teaching thing be to you.'

'I am a deaf man be, so what you say enters not my ears.'

'My spoken words you say do not enter your ears but your inside they have entered.'

'They will die,' said the black shoe man strongly.

'You say water has my inside entered. I know not whiteman's book. Their book learning is different from earth's knowledge which has come down from our ancestors. Book teaches not that. You say water has my inside entered. But you know not the power of water?

'Your eyes, don't they see the river? Your eyes,

don't they see the yams, coco-yams, sugar canes, plantains? Can they grow without the power of water? And what is behind the power of water? Without water can you in the world live? Water is soft but is it not the strongest thing be? My spoken words come out of the water in my inside.'

'You are not with your body,' scoffed the black shoe man.

'I am with my body.'

'If you are with your body saying this why not say it in front of Izongo?'

'In front of Izongo I will say this when the time is correct.'

'Why not say it today?'

'The rain never comes before its time.'

'You are all this saying because we have licked each other's blood.'

'Yes. I am all these things saying because of our oath. I cannot a bad thing do to you and you cannot a bad thing do to me. My inside told me I should all these things say to you because I am now a cup be which has been over-filled with water. All I am saying into your ears is simply water pouring over the sides of the cup.

They then walked in silence. The black shoe man, with the new black shoes hanging from his left hand walking like a man with a dead foot, now making detours over puddles and skipping palm kernel shells strewn on the ground to strengthen the ground; and the other never wishing to break contact with the ground walking over puddles and sharp palm kernel shells.

They silently walked with silence between them. Then the black shoe man suddenly stood still and held the other, stopping him.

'These words you speak are true but they have no shadow,' said he in a whisper.

'They may not now have power to create anything but before our time is finished or at the time of our born children, they may have power.'

'Then let us speak not of these things now. Let's leave it for the time of our children. We are speaking our breath away for nothing.'

'You think Okolo is the first to have these words grow in his inside? No. Just as you are trying to kill them, many there are who are the same thing doing. Nobody withstands the power of the spoken word. Okolo has spoken. I will speak when the time is correct and others will follow and our spoken words will gather power like the power of a hurricane and Izongo will sway and fall like sugar cane.'

'These words are not your words. They are the words of your father's father's father who they said knew everything,' said the black shoe man and started walking with silence.

'Nothing we can do, nothing!' The words burst out from his mouth after walking with silence for awhile. 'Our words will have no power.'

'Our words will have power when we speak them out. Let's wait till the time is correct. Okolo he has no wife, no children and his father and mother are dead. So he thinks nothing. So let us wait. When the time reaches, we will our work lose. Our children will know the root of it and will look after their mothers.'

'But you know what will happen to Okolo if he comes back.'

'Let's speak no more. A bad spirit has our insides entered.'

With this they walked with silence between them and one by one they called on the Elders and delivered their message.

As the messengers their message were delivering, inside the dark dark hut at the end of the town, Tuere and the cripple were talking with little flame from a little fire in the hearth showing only their two faces facing each other.

'What is the root of it?' Tuere asked as Ukule, the

cripple, told her of the celebration.

'No other root to it than to buy the insides of all the people. But things are softly softly happening under the ground.'

'What is it?' Tuere asked anxiously.

'You know the messengers?'

'Yes, go on.'

'The tall one, the son of the son of the son of Bumo, the wise one?'

'Yes, tell the story.'

'Okolo's words have in his insides grown.'

'How do you know?'

'They did not see me, but I heard their spoken words.'

'What did they speak?'

'The name of the tall one is Tiri.'

'Yes, I know, go on.'

'I see. I told you before Tiri is not like the others.'

'Yes. What did he say?'

'He says the money paid them by Izongo is bad money and that he, too, like Okolo will speak. Only he says the time is not correct yet.'

'Any more?'

'No more. They were about seeing me so I went into a house and I heard no more.'

Then silence fell between them with Tuere looking with all her shadow at the little flame burning with the spirit of fire. She looked at the little flame with all her shadow and Ukule, the cripple, looked at her face with his eyes straight like a pin boring into a body.

'If only Okolo would wait until the time is correct,' Tuere at last whispered to the flame.

'Yes, it is just like digging yam before harvest time,' Ukule, the cripple, said.

'Yes, but the yam has to be put in the waiting yam heap first. That's what Okolo is doing now. Let the words that have grown take root. That's what I am asking from the hand of Woyengi. Then nothing I will care, because whatever they do to Okolo is nothing, nothing!'

So Tuere and Ukule, the cripple, spoke with all their bodies and shadows bringing forth words and words before the little game burning with the spirit of fire; seeking, wishing, praying to Woyengi, who all things created, to make Okolo's words gather power before his returning time, knowing Okolo must to Amatu return since his umbilical cord was buried in the ground of the town.

SEVEN

The Elders came one by one to Izongo's house and when they had sat in a semicircle facing Izongo, Izongo called them each by their praise names as it is usually done at gatherings when something is to be discussed.

Izongo: *'One-man-one-face!'*

First Elder: 'Yes! No two persons have the same face, and no two persons have the same inside. What is yours?'

Izongo: 'You are asking me? I am *lightning*!'

First Elder: *'Lightning!'*

Izongo: 'Yes. I am *lightning*. Nothing stands before lightning. What is yours?'

Second Elder: 'You are asking me? I am *water*.'

Izongo: *'Water!'*

Second Elder: 'Yes! I am *water*. Water is the softest and the strongest thing be. What is yours?'

Izongo: 'What you say is correct. You are asking me? I am *he-who-keeps-my-head-under-water*.'

Second Elder: *'He-who-keeps-my-head-under-water!'*

Izongo: 'Yes! His cloth will also touch water.'

All Elders: 'Correct! Correct!'

Izongo: 'If only one person in this thing be, Okolo could have everything spoiled.'

All Elders: 'Yes! Yes!'

Izongo: 'What is yours?'

Third Elder: 'You are asking me? I am *fire*!'

Izongo: *'Fire!'*

Third Elder: 'Yes! He who touches me his fingers will burn! What is yours?'

Izongo: 'You are asking me? I am *pepper*.'

Third Elder: *'Pepper!'*

Izongo: 'Yes; I am *pepper*. Pepper hurts but without it food is tasteless. And what is yours?'

Fourth Elder: 'I am *bad waterside.*'

Izongo: '*Bad waterside!*'

Fourth Elder: 'I am! You will roll down if you are not careful. And yours?'

Izongo: 'You are asking me? I am *ant.*'

Fourth Elder: '*Ant!*'

Izongo: 'Many ants gather together and crumb bigger than themselves they carry.'

All Elders: 'Correct! Correct!'

Izongo: 'And yours?'

Fifth Elder: 'You are asking me? I am *if-it-were-me.*'

Izongo: '*If-it-were-me!*'

Fifth Elder: 'Never say so. Wait until what has to me happened has happened to you. What is yours?'

Izongo: 'You are asking me? I am *unless-you-provoke-me.*'

Fifth Elder: '*Unless-you-provoke-me!*'

Izongo: 'I will not provoke you if you don't provoke me. And yours?'

So Izongo called and answered praise names. He called them one by one until the last Elder was called and gave the wise meaning behind the names. When this he had done, Izongo with a loud voice called:

'O, Amatu!'

Elders all together: 'Yes!'

'In the town, is there no man or there is man?'

'There is man.'

'Any happening thing we can face?'

'We can do anything!'

Having made their shadows strong and formidable, having made them feel power to even empty the continually flowing river with their bare hands, Izongo told them the reason for calling them.

'Seven days have finished,' he began, 'since from our midst I . . . we cleared a stinking thing; and since then our breaths have reached ground. Is it not right that we mark this with a little celebration?'

'Yes, yes!' the Elders shouted.

'Well, my men,' he continued, 'I have decided that we celebrate today. So go tell all that they should gather here when the day is finishing. . . . Don't go yet,' he said as the Elders did as if to go at once.

'One small thing more. All of you will each kill a goat and bring it with a jar of palmwine.'

With this Chief Izongo stalked into his room and the Elders rose one after the other and left.

EIGHT

'Did he touch you?'

The daughter-in-law her hands clasping and unclasping in front of her opened not her mouth.

'Speak everything out now. If you everything speak out not, things of the ground will hold you. Do you this know?'

The daughter-in-law her hands clasping and unclasping opened not her mouth, standing in the centre of a circle of men and women. Her husband, sitting opposite her, opened not his mouth; the mother-in-law, sitting near her son, opened not her mouth but with words moving up her throat she her lips tightened and the imprisoned words creased her brows and made her breath like a running person's. The men were palmwine and beer drinking, palmwine and beer brought by the son of the mother-in-law, for it was he who called them on his mother's teaching words to find out the truth from his bride and to invoke things of the ground, if she spoke things that did not enter their insides.

'You, girl,' began the oldest man who was the questioning man. 'You, girl, you open not your mouth? We who are here are your fathers be and you are stepping on our heads by not opening your mouth to say yes or no. I know your father. He is a good man. I know your mother. She is a good woman. She hears what your father says. They are all good people be. Why put shame on their heads? You are from a good house. Why are you making yourself as if you are from a bad house? Is your head so strong that you cannot bow it to us, your Elders?'

'This time girls are not like us be when we were girls,' said a woman, and the mother-in-law her head slowly shook.

'Now the truth speak. Did he your body touch?'
asked the questioning man.

'Again and again I have said he did not touch me,'
said the daughter-in-law strongly. 'I have the straight
thing spoken but you say that is not the straight thing
be. Do you want me to say the thing that is not straight?
If what I have said does not enter your insides, let me
swear by the things of ground, things of the town and
swear by the dead. I have my body prepared.'

'Softly softly, speak,' scolded one man.

'You this time girls are not a bit good.'

'All your mouths close,' began the questioning man
with a wave of his hand. 'The girl here, she says Okolo
did not her body touch. So the only thing left is to
invoke the things of the ground and the things of the
town and the dead.' Then into his glass he poured fresh
palmwine and as he did so the brother of the girl stood
up.

'Wait,' he said, 'I have something here to say from
my inside.'

'Say it then,' said the questioning man stopping
pouring the palmwine.

'All of you open your ears and listen. This girl here,
Ebiere, my sister, we are from the same womb be and
we are of the same father be. So her hands and her feet
all belong to me. All her body belongs to me. Now
listen to what I have to say. You are treating her as if
nobody owns her. She has said Okolo her body did not
touch but it does not enter your insides.'

And so Ebiere's brother took her and went away and
the men and women their palmwine finishing, also
went away, leaving the mother-in-law and her son.

'I will marry her,' said the son almost in a whisper,
looking at the ground.

'What did you say?' said the mother looking at him
quickly.

'I said I will marry her,' he repeated quietly.

'Your spoken things do not enter my ear. How can

you a spoiled girl marry at this your young age? How can you a thing like that do with your hands, fingers, feet and toes all correct? How can you a thing like that do with your eyes all complete, your ears complete and not even deaf? Is your head not correct to think of marrying a spoiled girl? I think your head is not correct.'

'You brought her and said I should marry her, so I am marrying her,' was all her son said.

'Is it a bad thing be what I did?' the mother said standing up, and then sat back on her seat and lowering her voice said : 'Your father died and left us alone when even your first teeth had appeared not. Since then I have tried with my breasts and then my hands to see that you became a man. And now you a man be but you a wife need to be complete. Look son, I want a grandchild but not a grandchild from a spoiled girl. If you say you want to marry her, then find Okolo, bring him here and let him swear that he did not her body touch.'

To this the son opened not his mouth. He looked at the ground, he looked up at the sky. Then he looked at his fingers one by one.

'I did not want to marry before. But I like her now and I will marry her,' he said after a while.

'Then find Okolo,' urged his mother.

'Where can I see him in this Sologa?'

'The listening ones took him.'

The son scratched his head. 'I have no money to find him,' he said quietly.

'Money? You will take money to find him?' his mother asked not believing.

'Without money I can't find him. Money is inside everything in Sologa.'

Then the mother went into the house and came back. 'If so take this,' thrusting money into her son's hands, 'and find him,' she said and went back into the house. And the son thrusting the money into his pocket walked away.

NINE

'If only what?' Okolo asked his inside, but his inside said nothing. For silence had flooded it, driving away words, teaching words. So leaning on the thinking-nothing wall Okolo sat seeing only darkness, the kind of darkness you see when you close your eyes. Seeing only darkness in front like the wall. Okolo looked back at his early days when he was a small boy, a small boy going to the farm with his mother in a canoe and making earth heaps to receive the yam seedlings. How sweet his inside used to be when at the day's finishing time with the sun going down, they paddled home singing; and how at harvest time when the rain came down almost ceaselessly, they returned home with the first yams, only for small boys, like him, to eat first. How in expectation of the first yams he went through the long planting time . . . then the death of his mother and then his father. Then he remembered his father's spoken words when he was dying : 'I could have been a big rich man be,' his father had whispered with his last voice, holding Okolo's hand, 'if the straight thing I had not spoken, if the straight thing I had not done. But I have a sweet inside and clean as the eye of the sky. The world is changing and engine canoes and whiteman's houses have everybody's inside filled. But open your ears and listen, son. Let the words I am going to speak remain in your inside. I wanted you to know book because of the changing world. But whiteman's book is not everything. Now listen, son, believe in what you believe. Argue with no one about whiteman's God and Woyengi, our goddess. What your inside tells you to believe, you believe and, always the straight thing do and the straight thing talk and your spoken words will have power and you will live in this world even when you are dead. So do not anything fear if it is the straight thing you are doing or talking.'

Okolo's running thoughts were held by the opening door. He raised his head and coming in was an officer of the listeners and behind him, standing outside, was a group of people and in front of the group of people stood the mother-in-law.

Thoughts knocked each other down in Okolo's inside. He looked at the group again but the mother-in-law was there. He gathered his thoughts together in his inside and strengthened them and strengthened his body as one about to be thrown on the ground. But he saw nothing to fear.

'You know them?' asked the officer.

'Only the woman,' said Okolo.

Thereupon the officer turned to the group outside. 'You say you want to take him?' asked the officer. 'He is a madman be and if I in this city see him, you will enter into trouble.'

The mother-in-law and the men put their heads together and nodded their heads in agreement.

'A canoe is going tomorrow so we will send him back home,' said one of the men.

'You will go with them?' the officer turned and asked Okolo.

Okolo's inside became sweet and immediately turned bitter when reminded of the mother-in-law. But another voice told him that since he did not touch her body he should fear nothing.

'Yes, I will go with them,' said Okolo with a straight voice.

'Get up then and go,' said the officer with a strong voice as if to break even the wall.

Thereupon Okolo stood up from his seat and passed out of the door.

'If we see you again in Sologa, you will be taken to the asylum,' the officer said loudly as Okolo with the mother-in-law and the group of men moved away.

Night had fallen and in one of the unpaved streets in the slum areas of Sologa the darkness was more than darkness because it had been forgotten. In the forgotten street stood a house with corrugated iron sheet walls and roof held together with nails and sticks. And in the house, sitting round an oil lamp, were the mother-in-law and her son, Ebiere, the bride, and her brother and a group of men and old women.

And sitting apart in a corner was Okolo, waiting, listening to his inside.

'Without him can't we something do?' said one impatiently.

'Let's wait small,' said another.

'Go and call him,' said the impatient one.

'He will come. He worked overtime. Let us wait small,' said the patient one.

Then silence fell and the people were as still as the fallen silence.

'A dead man's shadow has entered this house,' said one.

Everybody at once began talking and laughing as if something had their insides sweetened. Then there was a knock and everybody stopped talking and turned their eyes on the door. The questioning one who questioned Ebiere the other day entered in his work clothes.

'Have you come?' asked one.

'Yes, from the work place.'

He then, with importance in front of him, found a place in the group and sitting, looked round and saw Okolo in the corner.

'Is he the one?' he asked.

'Yes, that's him,' said one.

'If so, let's start. I have not reached house, and hunger is holding me hard. Now, Okolo, did you not this girl's body touch?' he asked pointing at Ebiere, the bride, and looking at Okolo with eyes that wanted to see his inside. Okolo got up from his seat and into the circle of light moved.

'No. I did not her body touch. You ask her. She will

79

tell you if any part of her body I touched,' he said with a strong voice.

The questioning one smiled and said Ebiere would not have known in her sleep.

'Have you your body prepared to swear by Amadosu?' he asked.

'I know I did not her body touch, so I have my body prepared to swear by any god you say,' said Okolo as one who is saying the straight thing.

'Your inside is your box. We cannot open it and see what is inside. Only the gods can, so swear,' said the questioning one.

Okolo thereupon moved, with no fear in his inside, to the door, then to the dark dark night outside in the forgotten street and raised his right hand and began to swear :

'Hear, O Amadosu. Something has fallen on my head which I do not know how to remove. If I did the thing which they are putting on my head, show in the usual manner. Things of the ground, also, hear and the dead, also, hear!'

Okolo thus swearing entered the house and sat on his seat at the corner.

'Have you seen that my sister knows nothing?' said the bride's brother with smile smile in his mouth.

'Wait until she is about to deliver a child,' said the mother-in-law in a soft, strong voice. 'Yes, that is the time indeed when things of the ground and the dead will hold her and she will not be able to deliver unless she confesses.'

Nobody had ever been made to prove his innocence by swearing on a matter like this and Okolo sat in his corner asking his inside the bottom of it. And the answer came clear but nothing more he knew to ask or think. So he sat praying to Woyengi to put hand for him not to forget his father's voice in his inside coming from afar. It sounded louder and louder until thunder it became and drove all other voices from his inside.

TEN

The canoe was full with men, women and children going home. Every available space was occupied, not even a space to stretch his legs. So Okolo sat with his knees drawn up to his chin trying not to touch anybody's body. This little he had now learned. He smiled in his inside. But is it possible for your body not to touch another body, for your inside not to touch another inside, for good or for bad?

Is it possible to make your inside so small that nothing else can enter? Are spoken words blown away by the wind? No! Okolo in his inside saw. It is impossible not to touch another's inside. It is impossible to make your inside so small that nothing else can enter. Only the insides of men without shadows can nothing enter. And men without shadows are dead. What of spoken words? Spoken words are living things like cocoa-beans packed with life. And like the cocoa-beans they grow and give life. So Okolo turned in his inside and saw that his spoken words will not die. They will enter some insides, remain there and grow like the corn blooming on the alluvial soil at the river side. Is his meaning of life then to plant *it* in people's insides by asking if they've got *it* . . .?

Okolo then at the world, people of the world, looked, each sprawling in the canoe, each trying to make his or her inside sweet and to rest by making himself or herself comfortable not caring about the next person. The result? Quarrels. And the yielding ones he saw get squeezed until their bodies could take it no longer.

What is their meaning of life? No, they can't one meaning of life have. Each man to one meaning of life; each woman to one meaning of life. Each one has his

81

meaning of life. What is the meaning of life to Izongo?
Maybe Izongo knows no meaning of life. Maybe he is
in darkness groping and grabs out of fear at anything
that touches him. Many there are like Izongo with no
sense of direction like you are in a fog in a river. You
paddle round and round or go in the opposite direction until the fog clears or you are guided by voices
from the village. The difference only is that Izongo lost
in the fog guides those who are also lost in the fog, and
those in the village who, by their voices, want to guide
him.

How about the Big One of Sologa? What is his meaning of life be? Maybe he knows, maybe he does not.
Maybe he knows but sees it in a mirror and what he sees
is himself. And the whiteman, the superintendent of the
listeners? He is no different. Only his skin is white. He
was surprised that somebody like him, Okolo, could be in
search of *it*. Maybe the whiteman's father did not
teaching words say to him as his father had said to him.

Yes, each one has a meaning of life to himself. And
that is perhaps the root of the conflict. No one can
enter another's inside. You try to enter and you are
kicked out at the door. You allow another to enter your
inside and see everything in it, you are regarded as
one without a chest or as one who nothing knows . . .
Maybe he is wrong. There may be only one meaning in
life and everybody is just groping along in their various
ways to achieve it like religion – Christians, Moslems,
Animists – all trying to reach God in their various ways.
What is he himself trying to reach? For him it has no
name. Names bring divisions and divisions, strife. So
let it be without a name; let it be nameless. . . .

So Okolo for three days and three nights sitting with
his knees drawn up to his chin, talked in his inside
and in the end agreed with his inside that everybody has
or ought to have a purpose apart from bearing children and the sweetness of one's inside in the world is
in the fulfilment of that purpose. The only hard thing,

rather one of the two hard things, is knowing your purpose in this world. The other which is harder, is not to corrupt it after knowing what your purpose is. As for him, his purpose he knows. He will keep it clean as a virgin sheet of white paper. And to keep it so clean, he will keep his inside as clean as the sky.

ELEVEN

The drums were beating in Amatu. They had been beating bad rhythms since the finishing of the day and the night had fallen. It was a night that the moon did not appear and it was darkness, proper darkness. Still the drums continued to beat in the compound of Izongo. And the people continued to dance, the men and women knowing nothing, dancing like ants round a lamp hung on a pole. They continued to dance and drink and eat goat meat, for today was the day to remember the day Okolo left the town. And Izongo to mark this great day wore a black suit with brown shoes and on his head was a white pith helmet in the dark night.

The drums quickened their beat and the women danced Egene. The men danced Egene. The other women not dancing clapped their hands in rhythm with the drums. The drums beat faster still and they danced faster, for their insides had come down to their feet and they were like a rope about to break under a great tension. Then Izongo raised his hand. The drummers saw the hand but they could not their hands stop at once because their insides were in their hands. And when at last their drumming they were able to stop, the dancers continued to dance. The drum beats they continued to hear because the spirit did not leave them. When at last the spirit left them slowly, one by one, they stopped dancing one by one and laughed like people caught doing something which is not proper.

Silence at last fell on them like cold water and their eyes cleared. Izongo then rose quickly from his seat and stretching his hands forward shouted:

'Han. . . . Amatu!'

'Hee!' the people answered shaking the ground.

'Han. . . . Amatu! In the town, are there people or not?'

'There are people!' cried the people at the tops of their voices and shaking their fists.

'Can we face any happening thing?'

'We can face anything,' answered the people with all the strength in their voices.

'Beat the drums!' Izongo ordered and resumed his seat. The drums started to beat and the people started to dance.

In her hut at the end of the town Tuere sat with Ukule, the cripple, talking, listening to the drums. The fire was low and it was not a proper fire be. It was like a leper's fire.

'Amatu is lost,' said Tuere when Izongo's shouting she heard, strengthening the chests of the people.

'Yes, Amatu is lost,' said Ukule solemnly.

'Do you think Okolo will return?' said Tuere, thinking, afraid.

'You know he will come back,' said Ukule.

'I do not know what to think. Sometimes I do not my inside see clearly. My inside at times hides something from me. I have been thinking of him and I fear he will come back. And the bad thing they will do to him, I do not know.'

'What you came with from Woyengi will happen to you, whatever you do. So I do not fear. I asked Woyengi to make me a cripple, so I am a cripple. Whatever happens to you, you came with it from Woyengi.'

'What you say is correct. We cannot in this world ourselves recreate. If in this world we can recreate ourselves I would become a man. When I die I will return as a man.'

'I will continue to be a man, but not a cripple.'

'They have their singing started again.'

'Listen to the voices. They are like stinking things be, spoiling the air.'

'They are like the voice of a dead bad medicine-man buried in a good burial ground shouting to be removed, but let's not speak death words.'

'When it will come, it will come like the manatee which comes the day you do not think of it. So why –'

'Sssh! Listen!' Tuere stopped Ukule. 'Listen, I hear footsteps coming.'

They listened in silence. The footsteps came like water dropping fast on paper.

'Maybe somebody going to dance,' whispered Ukule.

'No, it cannot be. Somebody going to dance won't come this way.'

'Who can it be?'

'He has stopped at the door!'

At that moment the mat covering the door moved aside and a dim figure stood there hesitating.

'Tuere,' the figure called.

'Yes,' she answered in whisper whisper from the darkness in the corner of the hut. 'Don't stand there; come in quick,' she said.

'Why did you come back?' she asked when Okolo had the house entered. 'Why did you come?'

'I had to come. They did not want me in Sologa also. They would have put me in a mad house. So I had to come back. What is the bottom of their dancing?'

'They are remembering the day you left town.'

'Good.'

'Good?'

'Yes. I am going to meet him!'

'Don't go. They say they will send you away for ever and ever if you come back.'

'They cannot a thing do to me. The town is there gathered and I want to face him before their eyes. I want the people to hear my voice.'

'What kind of good will that do?'

'You are asking this? You are speaking thus?'

'My inside just now is like a whirlpool and I am dizzy. I know not what to think.'

'Go not,' said a big voice from the darkness of the hut.

Okolo quickly turned and faced the big voice. 'Who is that?' he asked.

'It is only Ukule. He is one of us.'

'It will not a good thing do for you to go,' continued Ukule. 'Palmwine has held them and they can do anything.'

'It is correct,' joined Tuere. 'They can do any bad thing with the eye of palmwine. Palmwine into their heads has climbed. So in their heads there is no room for any teaching words. Do not go, Okolo,' she pleaded.

'Am I then in this place to hide like a thief? Am I to run away? No! The straight word never runs away from the crooked word. I will go. They know not yet that I have come back. So when they see me, Izongo and the people will be surprised. Then I will ask Izongo and the Elders. Now I must go.'

With this Okolo turned and was about to move to the door when Tuere held him.

'Do not go,' she begged kneeling. 'Do not go. They will a bad thing do to you.'

'How do you know?' Okolo asked.

'I know. Your going does not agree with my body. Go not, Okolo, I beg, stay here.'

'I have my inside tied to this thing and I must go. I thank you for everything you have done for me. Thank you. Just hold yourself and stay here. I will come back.' Okolo then from the grip of Tuere freed himself gently and left.

When Okolo left thus Tuere stood there looking into the darkness.

'What will we do?' said Ukule coming out from the darkness in the corner.

Tuere did not hear him.

'I fear they will do him harm with the palmwine in their eyes.'

Tuere did not hear him. She just stood and then

87

suddenly turned and looking at Ukule said:

'Make the fire and tend it. I am coming.' And with this she left.

Izongo was passing the palmwine and the other drinks round. The sweetness of his inside passed sweetness. For the men and women had composed a praise song for him thus:

'Who can Izongo's words face?
Nobody!
Nobody!
Who can Izongo's place take?
Nobody!
Nobody!
Who gets money reach him?
Nobody!
Nobody!
Who is the leopard in town?
Izongo!
Izongo!
And who is goat in town?
Oko-lo!
Oko-lo!
Can goat fight leopard?
No, no!
No, no!'

As the people danced with the song and the palmwine in their heads, Okolo pushed his way through the crowd.

The people with their eyes on Izongo, the drummers, the dancers and the palmwine, had no eyes for Okolo. So they allowed him to pass with no alarm. He was now at the edge of the inner circle. He hesitated a bit, then ran towards the pole on which they hung the lamp.

The palmwine and the food had given Izongo sleep. So in the midst of all the drumming, singing, clapping of hands and stamping of feet, he was snoring. The Elders, too, the food and drink had given them sleep. So some with eyes closed and with mouths open slackly were trying to sing as the palmwine was being passed round. Even though with eyes only half open they took the palmwine and poured it into their mouths. Only one did not take palmwine and waved it away.

'Drink, man, drink,' said the palmwine bearer.

Abadi, who knew whiteman's book, only shook his head.

'If today you don't drink palmwine when are you going to drink? Will you die before you will palmwine drink?'

'What words are you speaking?' asked another palm-wine bearer who was going back to refill his jug.

'He says he palmwine wants no more.'

'Don't you know? Don't force him,' the second palmwine bearer said lowering his voice. 'He does not drink palmwine. We looked for beer, whisky, schnapps and brandy but couldn't get that. Palmwine does not fit him so leave him alone.'

So Abadi was left alone and the palmwine bearers went their ways, one continued to hand out palmwine and the other continued on his way to refill his jug.

As the palmwine bearers moved away Abadi yawned and looked at Izongo snoring, and at his fellow Elders sprawling on their seats.

Then he turned and looked at the men and women dancing, singing and laughing about like people whose heads are not correct. His eyes moved round the circle of dance and song until a running figure held them. He wiped his eyes and looked. The figure was now under the lamp. He half stood up, then sat. He wiped his eyes again and looked hard. Then he looked at Izongo and at the Elders. Izongo's eyes fluttered. He vigorously shook Izongo with one hand while the other shook the Elder near him. Izongo stopped snoring and slowly opened his eyes and yawning, asked:

'What is it?'

'Look!'

'Look what?'

'Okolo!'

'Where?' he asked with a jerk of his head, his eyes moving everywhere.

'Look under the lamp!'

'Aaahn ama!' Okolo's voice rang out from under the lamp on the pole. 'Aaahn ama!' he repeated as the people began to notice him. 'Aaahna ama!' he shouted again at the top of his voice.

As he thus shouted and the people saw him, the dancing stopped, the drumming stopped, the laughing stopped, all stopped at once and Izongo's body became stiff and strong like wood and his eyes became daggers pointed at Okolo. He gnashed his teeth, the sound of which was like that of a bone breaking under a dog's teeth. He gnashed his teeth. He looked at his Elders. Some were just being wakened, others sat trembling with their mouths opening and closing.

'You fools,' he hissed. 'What are you waiting for. Go and hold him,' he commanded with a strong voice.

Izongo's command shocked the Elders like an electric fish and they rushed towards Okolo. But a voice clear and cool like rain water hit them and they stopped short.

'Listen! Listen!' Tuere said as she walked fast to Okolo who had decided he had accomplished something by his mere reappearance and stood calm with the face of a god. As Tuere came to his side he looked at her with no surprise in his eyes.

'Listen!' she shouted as the Elders came to a stop. 'What is this big thing you want to put on your heads, you know-nothing people! Your insides are sick like sick eyes that cannot face light. . . .'

'Leave her to speak,' said Abadi, the educated one, as Izongo was about to rise in fury. And where Izongo sat back, he whispered something into his ears. Izongo's face cleared as that of a cat before a rat as Tuere continued to speak.

'. . . You fear every little thing, you are startled by

every little sound like one alone at night in the forest
is startled by every little sound. It is the fear in your
insides for one harmless man that is pushing you to do
this thing you want to do. You do not want to see him
for his merely asking if you have got *it*. . . .'

'I will stop her,' whispered Izongo angrily and made
to get up from his seat, but Abadi, the educated one,
stopped him.

'You cannot this thing do like that,' he said. 'There
is something which the whiteman calls "letting off
steam", that is allowing people to empty their insides
of grievances by talking. So let her and Okolo empty
their insides.'

'If the people see and they turn against us what will
we do?' Izongo said with fear creeping into his inside.

'Leave everything to me. Let her speak and allow her
to take Okolo with her. Then we continue the celebration.'

'What you speak does not enter my inside,' said
Izongo strongly.

'When everybody has gone then we shall put our
heads together. If an egg rolls against a stone the egg
breaks and if a stone rolls against an egg, the egg
breaks – so we shall talk. We are the stone be!'

'. . . We fear not the Elders,' Tuere's voice rang out
to the crowd. 'We fear no one. It is they who fear us
by fearing us they fear the straight thing. Now, I want
to ask you, Izongo and the Elders, have you got *it*?'

With this Tuere without another word Okolo's hand
held and walked away with the people making way for
them as they passed. Abadi stood up as Tuere left with
Okolo.

'Aaahn Amatu!' he shouted. There was only a scattered response and Izongo swept the crowd with his
eyes.

'Aaahn Amatu!'

'Hiimm,' the people responded as if suddenly roused
from sleep.

'Has the town any men or no men?'

'There are men,' shouted the people.

'Beat the drums, raise the song and let us continue,' shouted Abadi and sat down and Izongo nodded his approval. And so the drums they started to beat, the singers they started to sing and the dancers they started to dance. But the drums, the singers and the dancers were lifeless like soup without pepper and after a small time Izongo raised his hand to stop the celebrations. When everything stopped he stood up from his seat and without a word he left, followed by the Elders to their meeting place. And the people began to move away silent. The dancers and singers, their bodies became cold and they moved away, silent; and the drummers, their fingers became fingers of a shadow on a wall and they moved away and the drums lay silent, dumb.

TWELVE

Izongo with Abadi and the other Elders sat silent, after everybody to his house had gone, looking at the dead field where only a little while ago there was movement and life in the very dust that rose to the stamping feet. Thus they sat silent for a little while, when Izongo took a deep breath like one about to dive into the river and spoke slowly with finality behind every word :

'This is the time to show all that we can do what has come out of our mouths. This is the time to show everybody that we speak not words without shadows. What we say we will do, we will do.'

He then turned and looked at Abadi for the usual nod of the head, but Abadi today merely shifted on his seat as if himself to make more comfortable. Izongo looked at the other Elders and they responded with their usual nods of their heads. Izongo turned again to Abadi but Abadi's head was in his hands with his right foot tapping unseen, unheard. The other Elders craned their necks and looked at Abadi, particularly one by the name of Otutu who had been displaced by Abadi as Izongo's right hand man. He had, therefore, secretly kept a grudge in his inside for Abadi. And now that Abadi seemed, by his silence, to disagree with Izongo he strengthened his chest, stood up and spoke fast and loud as if for fear Izongo would stop him.

'We here on this side agree with what you say,' he said, addressing Izongo. 'What we say we will do, we will do. It has reached the time when we must something do to stop this thing. Any person who turns his back on what we all agreed we will do is a woman and is not fit to sit among us, the Elders of this famous town.

He should no longer put his mouth into our meetings. Our insides must be with the strength of iron. This is what has come out of my inside and I say no more.'

As Otutu spoke thus, Izongo's eyes moved back and forth between Otutu and Abadi. And when Otutu finished speaking what had come out of his inside and sat down, Izongo's eyes stayed on Abadi who had all the time remained with his head in his hands. There was silence, silence of questions and doubts surrounding Abadi. He at last raised his head with a jerk, stood up and spoke:

'As I sit here with my mouth closed does not mean that I have not got a strong inside or that what our leader has said does not enter my inside. A whiteman's parable says, "Look before you leap," and I was only looking into my inside to see how the whole problem is. And what I have seen is that what we all want is how to close Okolo's mouth. We have all agreed on one way which our leader has now asked us to carry out. Now I have seen that there are other ways of doing a thing. You know our people. I have something heard a few days ago. Not everybody danced and drank here tonight with his or her inside. If we now do what we said we would do, a big thing on our heads may fall which perhaps, like a falling house may bury us. Who then will become the victor? Okolo, Okolo whose mouth we want to close. So in order that this about-to-happen thing will not on our heads fall, I will go alone and speak to him. If I fail to make him see how today is, if I fail to wake him from his dream, then we will do what we said we would do if he showed his face again in this town. This is what I see.'

Jumping up from his seat Otutu shouted almost at the top of his voice.

'What our valuable second leader is saying is that we go and kneel before Okolo and beg him. I ask you,' turning to the Elders, 'have you ever heard of a thing like this?'

94

Some said no, a few others opened not their mouths. Otutu sat down a little disappointed at not receiving the full agreement he had expected from the Elders. He sat down muttering something to himself.

As his eyes moved back and forth between Abadi and Otutu Izongo's inside was turning furiously like a whirlpool. He had never heard two different words before at any of his meetings with the Elders. They had every time acted with their insides all as one. He looked at this never-happened-before thing from the ground to the sky. How Abadi spoke seemed he was about to throw his back on him. Abadi had always given him his inside, but now, it seemed, he had a different thing in his inside.

'What is the bottom of this?' he asked himself. Even some of the Elders opened not their mouths. 'What is the bottom of this?' he again asked himself. The bottom must be Okolo. Since Okolo came nothing but troubles and difficulties which he had to place his eyes on his occiput to overcome. Okolo therefore must go.

As Izongo was thinking thus his eyes were moving from Abadi to Otutu and from Otutu to Abadi. Then as Otutu sat down muttering to himself he got up and spoke standing straight.

'I am Chief Izongo. My name, like the wind, has reached everywhere, has entered everybody's ears. And people know me as one who always does the straight thing and that is doing what has come out of my mouth. I said with all our insides joined together that if Okolo in this town showed his face again he would from the town be driven away for ever. He came back today beating his chest. We will, therefore, beat our chests and carry out what we had ourselves agreed we would do.'

He paused and looked at each Elder with his eyes shining in the night like a leopard's. Then suddenly his voice rang out.

'You go and prepare the canoe,' at one of the Elders pointing with fingers shaking. 'What are we waiting for? Let's go and get them.'

With this he ran towards Tuere's hut followed by all the Elders but Abadi whose face was now like one taking nivaquine.

Tuere still Okolo's hand gripping entered her hut and Okolo followed like one who knows not what to do with himself. Inside, Ukule, the cripple, sat by the fire waiting silent. Okolo and Tuere silent stood. They stood with silence, only breathing they were hearing. They stood thus awhile then Okolo said, letting fall a deep breath :

'They will come to get me. So let me go to them. I do not want them to touch you.'

At this Tuere, too, let fall a big breath and said : 'Let them come and take us. I have been dead many many years. So I fear no more. From this standing moment, wherever you go, I go.'

Then turning to Ukule she said, 'You go and leave us. You stay in the town and in the days to come, tell our story and tend our spoken words.'

Thereupon Ukule moved and when he reached the door turned and said, 'Your spoken words will not die.' With this he moved into the outside darkness.

When day broke the following day it broke on a canoe aimlessly floating down the river. And in the canoe tied together back to back with their feet tied to the seats of the canoe, were Okolo and Tuere. Down they floated from one bank of the river to the other like debris, carried by the current. Then the canoe was drawn into a whirlpool. It spun round and round and was slowly drawn into the core and finally disappeared. And the water rolled over the top and the river flowed smoothly over it as if nothing had happened.